A BOND OF DESTINY

THE UNHEARD SYMPHONY: SILENT HARMONIES OF A NATION'S TRANSFORMATION

INDURKHYA MANISH

To,
My beloved mother,

Smt. Rekha Gupta

Whose timeless wisdom and unvavering love continue to guide and illuminate my path beyond this world and into eternity.

Contents

Threads of Destiny

"Beyond these threads of fate and fight,
We can stand unbound in the coming light."

Social stratification and hierarchy are not merely by-products of collective efforts in social development; they are integral to social evolution, continuously changing their form over time and circumstance. The division of labour, the cornerstone of our collective progress, has enabled societies to build strength and endure adversity. Yet, as humanity advanced, an inherent yearning for distinction emerged, driven by ego and the desire for material and psychological supremacy. This natural process gradually solidified into rigid class boundaries. What began as a mechanism for organising work soon evolved into entrenched systems, such as castes, that restrict the free flow of ideas and interactions, resulting in a closed system that hinders development. While the division of labour remains essential for progress, inflexible social barriers weaken our collective resilience and expose society to forces that can unravel its unity.

In this environment of societal views and biases, a remarkable story emerges from the Indian subcontinent as it nears independence—a country grappling with its identity. In a small village in Uttar Pradesh, two youths, Ramveer and

Chinmay, form an unexpected friendship that challenges long-standing restrictions. Ramveer, born into a *Dalit* family long marginalised by social prejudice, finds his destiny intertwined with that of Chinmay, the son of a progressive landlord named Shivraman. Their friendship, nurtured through shared struggles and the pursuit of education, becomes the seed from which a profound reimagining of identity and ambition grows.

As Ramveer and Chinmay navigate a complex academic landscape, they encounter the promise of newfound opportunities and the resistance of deeply rooted prejudices. Constitutional reservations open doors for Ramveer yet simultaneously expose him to the multifaceted challenges of transcending a system designed to confine him. A pivotal moment arises when Ramveer, driven by an absurd personal comment from a colleague who questioned his abilities and right to the reserved seat, chooses to forgo these benefits. In a desperate bid to secure his friend's future, Chinmay covertly alters Ramveer's application for the Indian Civil Service—a gesture that, while intended to safeguard his future, sows the seeds of lingering guilt and transforms their once-unbreakable bond.

Decades later, at the cusp of the nation's most severe economic crisis, the echoes of that early act of defiance resonate with fiery intensity. The reformist spirit embodied by Ramveer and Chinmay now drives bold structural and functional changes—an extraordinary testament to the resilience of human conscience and its remarkable capacity for positive change. Their intertwined destinies serve as a poignant exploration of the complexities of social mobility, personal integrity, and the enduring power of human conscience. They also lay the foundation for millions to understand the truths of social Inclusion from ancient epics to the modern constitutional framework.

This gripping narrative invites readers from all corners of the globe to delve into the intricate dynamics of the caste system, examining the relationship between personal ambition and collective advancement and the unwavering pursuit of self-determination. It illustrates the delicate interplay between economic renewal and social change, where each aspect challenges and supports the other in the relentless quest for a fair and thriving society. Through the evocative experiences of Ramveer and Chinmay, we witness not only the trials faced by a society in flux but also the timeless struggle to break free from the constraints of history, culture, religious beliefs, and the profound complexities of human conscience. What new paths will emerge as these two friends challenge the status quo, and how will their story resonate with the world at large?

CHAPTER I

The Seeds of Rebellion: A Birth Leads, a Tumult

The monsoon rains arrived as a long-awaited blessing this season, gifting the fields of Ratanpur village in southern Uttar Pradesh with the promise of an abundant harvest. The life-giving downpours transformed the landscape, saturating the parched soil and nurturing the crops that sustain the community. With each raindrop, the earth exhaled a rich perfume of renewal, filling the air with hope and vitality that permeated every mud-brick dwelling. The monsoon represents more than just a change in weather; it symbolises sustenance, prosperity, and, indeed, the vital lifeblood of a village that depends on its bounty.

As dawn's gentle light spilt over the horizon, the fields stirred with the quiet industry of farmers and labourers, their movements a symphony of toil and hope. *Gadarias,* a caste that shepherded cattle, goats, and sheep flocks, started guiding their herds to pasture. *Lohars,* the blacksmiths, forged and shaped metals, while *Kumhars* (Potters) coaxed clay into vessels of surprising grace. Many men and women from the *Dalit* (Untouchables) community left their huts to work in the fields. The *Kshatriyas* struggled to uphold their traditions, and the *Brahmins* were engrossed in religious rituals and pursuits related to education. A handful of *Vaishy families* (Traditional Traders caste) managed the village's modest commerce, dealing in everything from necessities to luxury items.

On the surface, the village appeared tranquil—within its earthen boundaries, it thrived as a diverse tapestry of communities that unknowingly embodied Mahatma Gandhi's vision of *Gram Swaraj*. However, centuries-old social, religious, economic, and cultural prejudices had tightly ensnared the very fabric of this tapestry, binding it so firmly that people had come to embrace it as their destiny.

With the rise of new empires, tax-driven policies rendered land levies increasingly unbearable. This relentless agricultural taxation drained the lifeblood from the poorest farmers and artisans. Repeated invasions and plunder, predating even the *Delhi Sultanate*, had already sapped the wealth of local landlords and princely estates. From the revenue-hungry *Mughal Mansabdari* to the harsh land reforms under British colonial rule, every successive regime tightened the noose in its pursuit of profit. With each increment in agrarian taxes, the cycle of poverty and subjugation deepened, widening the chasm of inequality, much like how, today, corporations try to shift the burden of financial losses onto the lowest-paid workers. The insatiable ambitions of rulers gradually ensnared the most vulnerable and voiceless into a relentless spiral of deprivation and oppression.

Separated from the nearest railway station by almost thirty kilometres of treacherous dirt roads that dissolved into mud lakes during monsoons, Ratanpur existed in its self-contained universe. News of the world beyond filtered in through monthly or fortnightly magazines, journals, and occasional newspapers that found their way only to Shivraman's doorstep, carried by the postman. He was an educated man standing at the crossroads of tradition and transformation; his wire-rimmed spectacles and voracious reading habits made him different from his upper-caste peers.

Though not tall, Shivraman's presence was impossible to ignore. At forty-two, his poised demeanour, fair complexion, and striking features lent him an air of quiet dignity. Ever watchful and curious, his deep brown eyes registered every subtle change—the gentle turn of the seasons, the murmur of distant political shifts, and the silent suffering of those left at the margins. Yet, bound by his modest trader roots, his keen insights often fell on deaf ears, overshadowed by the ignorance of a narcissistic upper class and the neglect faced by the *Dalits* and the backwards castes.

During the tumultuous era of the Second World War, when every nation seemed ensnared in a relentless storm of conflict, the Congress, with fiery resolve, launched the proactive Quit India Movement—unleashing a surge of high energy that swept across the country like a tidal wave—Ratanpur stood apart, serene and untouched. Nestled in its remote embrace, the village lay almost in a state of *Yog Nidra*, its tranquil slumber undisturbed by the roaring chaos of war and rebellion echoing beyond its borders.

A humble, clean hut stood at the edge of the village, where a worn path led to endless fields, distinguishing it from the surrounding huts—the home of Budhai and Tulsa, a Dalit couple. Their lives, steeped in labour from dawn until dusk, were etched into every calloused line of their hands and every bowed spine. They had toiled in the fields and served in the grand households of the upper caste, their existence marked by an unyielding legacy of oppression and hardship.

Budhai was a man of few words and many sorrows. At thirty, he appeared forty, his face weather-beaten and creased with lines that spoke of generations of struggle. What distinguished him was an unflinching honesty that refused to bow, even when his back was against the wall. He carried himself with quiet dignity, which some mistook for insolence. After a Long struggle as an agricultural labourer under many masters, he finally earned Shivraman's unwavering recognition.

Tulsa radiated a different kind of courage—a blend of meticulous determination and unyielding spirit. Slender, despite the trials of two pregnancies, her eyes shone with a brilliant mix of creativity, common sense, and industriousness, illuminating her deft management of agriculture and household affairs. While many upper-caste women sought her services for guidance, she found herself comfortable with Janki Devi, the generous wife of Shivraman, whose supportive nature further enriched the tapestry of their intertwined destinies.

This couple's unflagging diligence and untarnished integrity caught the eye of Shivraman, the village's wealthy intellectual, who provided them steady employment throughout the changing seasons.

On a humid August night, while cries of "Angrejo Bharat Chhodo"—British, Quit India!—resonated across the nation, Tulsa, unaware of this, brought a son into the world. A Distant relative of Tulsa, Imarti, had worked through the night, her experienced hands guiding the stubborn infant into the world while Budhai paced outside, wearing a path in the packed earth with a few of his relatives.

A son!" Imarti finally declared, stepping out of the hut, her greying hair damp with sweat. "The gods have blessed you with a strong boy!"

For Budhai, this moment was as unexpected as it was overwhelming. In his world, the belief ran deep—true salvation, *moksha*, could only be attained if a son performed the final rites. And now, fate had finally answered his silent prayers.

He arrived after two daughters, Meera and Savitri, girls with their mother's quick mind and their father's stubborn pride, a blessing they had wished for many years.

They christened him Ramveer—the brave—a name heavy with expectation and hope.

As Tulsa cradled her newborn son, made from an old, torn sari, her exhausted face illuminated by the dancing flame of an oil lamp that cast more shadows than light, she whispered her wishes for the little new guest.

"You will not bow, my son," she murmured against his downy head. "You will not crawl where others walk. You will stand tall even if it means standing alone."

This was more than maternal affection speaking; this visionary dreamt of prosperity for her children while standing knee-deep in poverty.

Janki Devi entered the study, her anklets announcing her presence with gentle chimes. At thirty-five, she retained the beauty of her youth, though the responsibility of four kids had etched fine lines around her expressive eyes. Unlike many women of her generation, she could read and write, having been taught by Shivraman himself in the early years of their marriage—a radical act in a community where female literacy was viewed as unnecessary at best and dangerous at worst.

She announced, "Tulsa has delivered a son," by the same evening, arranging a brass tray with steaming tea and salty snacks for Shivraman.

Shivraman looked up from his reading, removing his spectacles and pinching the bridge of his nose to relieve the strain of early morning study. "That is good news indeed. We should send something if they require any help."

Janki Devi paused, carefully measuring her words. "I've already prepared a basket with ghee, rice, and jaggery. And the green sari I no longer wear." She hesitated.

"Budhai has named him Ramveer," announced Mohan, the eldest son of Shivraman, as he returned from Budhai's hut after delivering some essential items following lunch. His voice carried a weight of significance beyond a mere birth announcement. "Budhai wishes to celebrate with a *Nautanki* performance."

Janki Devi's hands froze mid-stitch, her embroidery forgotten as she looked up with eyes widened in disbelief. "A *Nautanki*? For a *Dalit* child's birth? The village will not countenance such a thing."

Their eldest son, Mohan, a serious twelve-year-old with his father's intellectual curiosity and his mother's practical nature, looked in the eye of his mother with curiosity. "Why shouldn't they celebrate in their community? It's our decision whether we join that or not."

"That's different," interjected Janki Devi, "But this was never a tradition, and I have never heard a *Dalit* family celebrate the birth in such a way in any village in last so many years," she trailed off, suddenly aware of his husband's piercing gaze, who has somewhat liberal attitude deep-rooted caste system.

News of the *Nautanki* celebration on a *Dalit* child's birth spread through the village with the swiftness of flame through dry grass, igniting outrage among those who considered themselves keepers of tradition.

The reaction varied across castes: Brahmins spoke sacrilege of holy traditions; Kshatriyas muttered about order and discipline, while those of the lower castes watched with a mixture of trepidation and hope, wondering if they were witnessing the first cracks in a system that had confined them for centuries.

By the following evening, a contingent of young men led by Pandit Ramakant—the village Brahmin whose lineage had for generations served as custodians of sacred rituals—arrived at Shivraman's threshold, as he was an employer of the *Dalit* family. Their faces etched with indignation,

Pandit Ramakant, despite his title, was barely forty, with a perpetual scowl that had earned him the secret nickname *"Jwala"* among the village youths. His authority derived not from wisdom or compassion but from a meticulous adherence to ritual and an encyclopaedic knowledge of various Sanskrit religious texts, which only a few in his caste and no one in another knew.

The confrontation unfolded in the courtyard beneath the ancient banyan tree, its sprawling canopy a silent witness to countless village disputes. The tree predated even the oldest living resident, its aerial roots having descended to form additional trunks, creating a natural pavilion where village councils had traditionally gathered.

"This is nothing short of sacrilege," Ramakant proclaimed, his voice resonating with the authority of scripture. "These people aspire to transcend their divinely ordained station. Today they planned a *Nautanki* for on a birth; tomorrow, they will seek entrance to our temples and access to our wells!"

Several young men standing behind him nodded vigorously, their eyes ablaze with the zeal peculiar to those who mistake inherited prejudice for divine righteousness.

And then, a very low voice from the shadows challenged. It was Mohan, Shivraman's eldest, who had positioned himself on the periphery of the gathering. What catastrophe would follow if they were to celebrate a play at the ground of our village?

Ramakant's eyes narrowed dangerously. "Mind your place, boy. This matter is between your father and the village elders only because Budhai serves your family."

"Stopped his son from speaking anything further," Shivraman interjected smoothly, emerging from the house to stand beneath the banyan's spreading limbs.

Shivraman listened patiently, his hands clasped behind his back, his countenance revealing nothing as Ramakant continued his tirade about tradition, pollution, and the imminent collapse of cosmic order. When Ramakant finally fell silent, a hush descended upon the courtyard, broken only by the whispered conversation between banyan leaves and the evening breeze.

"And what catastrophe would unfold if they organise a play in their community?" Shivraman finally responded, his voice gentle yet crystalline in the gathering dusk.

Our contemporary institutions and organisations of renaissance Arya Samaj, Brahmo Samaj, Congress and RSS are actively propagating for the inclusion of Dalits and the backwards."

Ramakant's expression darkened like monsoon clouds before a deluge. "You speak blasphemy, Shivraman. These matters are ordained by Dharma, by-laws predating our existence by millennia."

"I speak of dharma in its truest sense," Shivraman countered, leaning slightly forward. His voice took on the cadence of a teacher explaining a simple concept to a particularly obstinate student.

He paused, taking a balanced and humorous tone. Did our most revered Lord Rama not partake of berries that the untouchable Shabari first tasted? If so, who is correct? Who is the crusader of Dharma? Is it Lord Ram or Pandit Ramakant Shastri who worships Lord Rama and justifies the opposite track?"

A collective gasp rippled through the gathering at what felt dangerously close to blasphemy. Even Ramakant appeared momentarily speechless, his mouth opening and closing silently, like a fish suddenly pulled from the water.

Shivraman knew his position was less potent in this gathering, so he lowered his voice. "Panditji, I am speaking about the same path our beloved Lord Rama and Krishna followed. The scriptures are not only for reciting mantras in Sanskrit; they also guide us in our way of life."

"This is not about scriptures only," Pandit Ramakant finally managed to put himself in some practical mode, his voice quavering with suppressed rage. This is about order. Remove one stone from the foundation, and the entire structure collapses."

Perhaps," Shivraman said, his voice carrying an air of quiet defiance, "some structures must fall if they can no longer bear the winds of change. Otherwise, their sudden collapse will bring devastation—one neither you nor I are prepared for."

Shivraman's children and Janki Devi watched from the window of their house, their expressions a mix of awe and trepidation. The air was tense, the weight of unspoken truths pressing upon the gathering. Sensing the conversation moving toward dangerous waters, Janki Devi whispered to Mohan, instructing him to call Shivraman and offer their guests refreshments.

It was a subtle but urgent reminder—within the family, boundaries mattered. Shivraman turned back to the gathering with a bureaucratic tone. "For me, there is no harm to Dharma if a *Dalit* celebrates a *Nautanki* play within their community. India stands at the threshold of independence—should we not extend its promise to all? Moreover, you are respected scholars who can act appropriately if this is an offence."

His words cut through the murmurs, striking at the heart of an unspoken caste rigidity. For centuries, social order had been upheld like an iron fortress, and even now, as colonial rule waned, old hierarchies resisted erosion.

"Please, let them carry on with their *Nautanki* as planned," he implored. "We might choose to step aside—the winds of change sweeping across this nation will spare Ratanpur no longer. We may yield gracefully or be shattered by them, but we can never hope to arrest their relentless advance."

As the gathering reluctantly dispersed, only a few men remained—Ramakant, the village priest, his eyes dark with unvoiced reproach.

"You have made dangerous enemies today, Shivraman," he murmured.

Shivraman's smile was wistful, not triumphant. I would have made many friends, Panditji, instead. This village—this land—is vast enough for all of us if only we set aside the fears that bind us to the prejudices."

Ramakant's voice was sharp. "This is not about fear. It is about respect—respect for our ancestors and the wisdom that has built our society.

Shivraman exhaled, his gaze distant. "Our ancestors were wise, yes. But they were also men of their time, shaped by the limits of their world. If we truly honour their memory, should we not evolve rather than merely exist within the walls they built?"

Ramakant shook his head, his expression unreadable. "You always have an excuse for everything, Shivraman. But words are not mere wind. Remember this: actions have consequences. With that cryptic warning, he departed, his disciples trailing behind him like shadows fleeing before the sun.

The *Nautanki* was held the following week—modest by upper-caste standards yet unprecedented for a Dalit family. No upper caste, including Shivraman and his family, had attended, as this was a celebration for the Dalit community. No one from a higher caste can imagine participating in any event or celebration, or else they would inevitably fall victim to the collective disregard of the upper castes.

The performers erected a simple stage on the village outskirts, near the cluster of *Dalit* dwellings, transforming the humble clearing into a space of unexpected magic. Saree fabrics hung from bamboo poles, creating a festive canopy where musicians tuned their instruments while actors applied elaborate makeup.

The performers enacted the legend of *Raja Harishchandra*, the sovereign who sacrificed everything at the altar of truth—a narrative choice pregnant with symbolism. The actor playing Harishchandra, majestic in his cardboard crown and silk robes, delivered his lines with such conviction that even the most sceptical viewers found themselves drawn into the ancient tale.

"Truth alone prevails in the end!" he proclaimed during the climactic scene, his voice carrying across the hushed audience. "Not wealth, not power, not the accident of birth—only adherence to truth can elevate a soul!"

Seated in the front row with baby Ramveer cradled in her arms, Tulsa wept silent tears—not of sorrow but overwhelming gratitude. Beside her, Budhai sat straight-backed and dignified, his expression betraying no emotion save for the occasional suspicious moisture in his eyes during particularly moving scenes.

The village remained fractured throughout the performance, with the upper castes boycotting the celebration. However, they did not take severe action against this, as Shivraman intelligently presented facts during the confrontation. Meanwhile, *Dalits* attended with a curious amalgam of apprehension and wonder, unaccustomed to seeing one of their own honoured so publicly.

Yet a few families of the lower castes—now referred to as the Backward Classes—arrived quietly, settling on the fringes, where they could watch from the shadows, unseen and unremarked.

When the performance concluded well past midnight, the actors received the customary applause and an outpouring of emotion most of them had witnessed. For many of the *Dalits* present, this marked the first time they had participated in a social celebration rather than being marginalised at a public gathering—the first time their joy had been deemed worthy of celebration rather than suppression.

As music and vibrant costumes transformed the ordinary night into something magical, little Ramveer slumbered peacefully in his mother's protective embrace, blissfully oblivious to the social turbulence his arrival had catalysed.

After years of harmony and peaceful living, this unprecedented incident carved a profound chasm between the *Dalits and the upper caste*. In the following days, subtle changes rippled through the village's social fabric: labourers were unexpectedly turned away from work at upper-caste households.

This small yet significant incident sparked a whirlwind of potential energy, charged with the simmering tensions between the upper castes and Shivraman's family. Ironically, this turmoil fostered a newfound respect among the Dalits, creating a subtle yet profound recognition of their dignity and defiance in the face of adversity.

As the winds of change began to sweep through the village, youth from the privileged castes found themselves drawn by a hidden agenda. They sought to challenge Shivraman's intellect, believing that by aligning themselves with the freedom movement, they could elevate their social standing against the expertise of Shivraman, which evolved in many years of continuous involvement and communication with different modern institutions, offered a platform, inviting these young men into rare ideological discussions that stirred curiosity and ambition.

This engagement led to a slow yet palpable awakening within the village. For many upper-class youths, it became an eye-opening experience that exposed them to the currents of social transformation pulsating through the nation's heart. As they navigated these ideological waters, the seeds of change began to sprout, rooted in the rich legacy of the Indian Renaissance and promising to reshape the village's future.

As the Quit India Movement gained momentum across the nation, it gradually absorbed the passion of many young villagers and subtly altered their convictions. The once-quiet lanes of Ratanpur now reverberated with the revolutionary slogan "Angrejo Bharat Chhodo"—a sign of political awakening in a place that had slumbered too long.

Young men who had previously concerned themselves only with seasonal harvests, matrimonial prospects, and prejudices now debated national politics with unexpected fervour. Some even travelled to neighbouring towns to hear speeches by Congress representatives, returning with pamphlets and newfound vocabulary that transformed the village's political discourse.

Years passed, and the lines drawn by that fateful celebration remained untouched; upper-caste people rarely visited Shivraman's home, unwilling to associate with a man who had so publicly challenged the social order. A remarkable silence surrounded his family—not the silence of obscurity but the pointed silence of deliberate exclusion. However, this led to the active participation of youth in various movements that gradually struck the rigid caste consciousness, at least beyond village boundaries.

Shivraman and his family observed these changes quietly, avoiding aggression or conflict. Although the initial turmoil subsided, a political transformation began amidst the village's upper class, subtly influenced by the soft winds of change. Over time, a social reformation emerged, confronting even the most deeply ingrained prejudices within Ratanpur's hierarchy and laying the groundwork for broader social transformation.

CULTURAL & CONTEXTUAL GLOSSARY:

Yog Nidra is a state of deep relaxation and conscious awareness between waking and sleeping.

Dalit: A term used in India to refer to historically marginalised communities under the caste system. They were formerly called 'untouchables.'

Brahmin: The highest caste in the traditional Hindu varna system, historically associated with priesthood and scholarship.

Kshatriya: The warrior and ruling caste in the Hindu varna system, traditionally responsible for military and administrative duties.

Nautanki: A popular form of folk theatre in North India characterised by colourful costumes, lively music, and dramatic storytelling; often used as a medium to express social and cultural narratives.

Quit India Movement: A pivotal campaign initiated in 1942 by the Indian National Congress demanding an end to British colonial rule in India, symbolising a significant surge in the nation's struggle for independence.

Rashtriya Swayamsevak Sangh (RSS) is India's prominent social and cultural organisation. It was established to unite people and foster a sense of nationalism.

Lagaan: A type of agricultural tax levied on agricultural land by various rulers and colonial powers.

Moksha: A transcendent state referring to being free from the cycle of birth, death, and rebirth.

Delhi Sultanate: A series of Islamic dynasties that ruled over a large part of the Indian subcontinent from the 13th to the 16th century.

Raja Harishchandra: A legendary king from Hindu Culture who sacrificed everything to uphold his word, even his kingdom and family.

Mughal Mansabdari: a hierarchical administrative and military structure where individuals were granted a "mansab" (rank) for Administration, Revenue collection, and Military Management.

VILLAGE SCHOOL

CHAPTER II

The Youngest Satyagrahi

Six monsoons passed, each resonating with calls for independence. However, life remained steadfast—economic, social, and cultural traditions continued their uninterrupted rhythm, and the silent bonds of caste stayed strong. Regardless of their affiliations with different organisations, local youths achieved nothing in their attempts to humiliate Shivraman and his family. Shivraman and his family, constantly vigilant, effectively upheld their status, rendering any challenges from the youths ineffective.

At the same time, groups such as the Indian National Congress, the Brahmo Samaj, the Ramakrishna Ashram, and Rastriya Swayamsevak Sangh promoted their ideas for socio-cultural reform alongside other movements focused on social integration. However, progress was deliberate and gradual due to the complexities of the deeply entrenched caste system, which has many layers of entanglement: social, economic, cultural, and religious.

On a golden afternoon in late September, when the first breath of autumn cooled the air after months of oppressive heat, the youngest son of Shivraman, Chinmay, sat beneath the largest mango tree in his father's orchard —a secluded spot he had chosen for his lesson. The boy traced verses with slender fingers, his lips moving in silent recitation. Unlike his elder brothers, who preferred playing indoor games like Playing Cards, Chess, and Ludo after school,

Chinmay found solace in solitary pursuits, his mind a fertile ground for poetry and logical contemplation. The poetry book in his lap was a gift from his maternal uncle, who was somewhat more affectionate towards his sister's youngest child.

A rustling at the edge of the orchard drew Chinmay's attention. A small, filthy boy, perhaps six years old, stood watching him with undisguised fascination. The child was lean yet resilient, his small frame hinting at hardship and endurance. His broad, searching eyes, set in a face streaked with dust, held a quiet intensity—far too knowing for someone so young.

Chinmay knows this child and has seen him often outside his home with Tulsa. Tulsa usually supports his mother with household work outside their home, as they are not allowed inside upper caste homes beyond the veranda.

"Are you hiding?" Chinmay asked, closing his book.

"No, just listening to your poem. The way you recite it is full of melody—please continue", the filthy boy replies in a very confident and clear tone.

Chinmay smiled at the admiration. "Do you know what it means? Can you read?"

Another head shakes, but the boy steps forward with surprising boldness instead of retreating. "I'm Ramveer. My mother works for your family." He paused, then added with quiet determination, "Will you teach me? I want to recite it the way you do."

Had an adult been present, they would have gasped at the audacity—a *Dalit* child requesting education was unthinkable. But Chinmay, who had many teachers at home and school, always aspired to dictate an inner psyche of being recognised.

"Come sit," he said, patting the ground beside him, unwittingly issuing an invitation that defied thousands of years of social convention.

Ramveer hesitated momentarily before settling cross-legged beside Chinmay, carefully maintaining a small gap between them—a habit ingrained by watching his mother maintain similar distances from her employers.

Chinmay's voice rose first in gentle verse, with Ramveer joining soon after, and together they savoured the poetry's rhythm late into the evening at Corus.

By the time shadows had lengthened across the orchard, they had progressed through several poems, Ramveer absorbing each with an intensity that surprised his young teacher.

"You must go before my brother comes looking," Chinmay said reluctantly, noticing the sun's position. "But come tomorrow, and we'll continue with more books of alphabets and numbers."

This marked the beginning of a delicate bond, a gentle connection meant to become part of the fabric of companionship. In the days to come, it would not only shape the nature of friendship and fellowship but also relentlessly confront the rigid structure of Ratanpur's longstanding social hierarchy, shaking its very foundations with the subtle strength of something timeless.

Your memory is impressive, and your pronunciation has improved significantly! Chinmay exclaimed a few months later, genuinely impressed as Ramveer recited all the verses, alphabets and numbers he'd taught him. They sat by the stream that marked the border of Shivraman's lands, their feet dangling in the cool water—another unconscious transgression of unwritten rules.

Over the changing seasons, their meetings expanded beyond lessons. They explored the countryside together, plucking many berries and plums from the outskirts, and discussed many snippets of conversations overheard at home. The onlookers perceived Ramveer as merely extending assistance, much like his father, a humble aide. Yet, the bond among these young children was far more profound—it was sculpting new dimensions of intellect and wisdom. While one found psychological fulfilment in teaching and explaining, the other derived joy from grasping new concepts, unravelling the questions they sparked, and committing them to memory.

As time unfurled its relentless course, their exchanges turned ever more frequently to a man named Gandhi—his enigmatic philosophy of Satyagraha, a quiet yet unyielding force; whispers of independence shimmering on the horizon; and the nascent dream of a new India rising from the ashes of the old. Ramveer drank in every word, his mind a crucible of rapt fascination, committing each detail to memory—a honed instinct of survival, born from the legacy of those long denied the permanence of the written word.

"What is Satyagraha exactly?" Ramveer asked one day as they sat perched on a high branch of the banyan, legs dangling in the breeze.

"I'm not sure," Chinmay admitted. My father often talks about it. Let's ask my brother Mohan. He's studying in the tenth standard now and must know about it."

A few days later, they cornered Mohan behind the family cowshed, away from the prying eyes of adults who might question why the young master was consorting with a *Dalit* child.

"Satyagraha?" Mohan repeated, pleased to display his knowledge. "It means 'holding firmly to the truth.' Gandhi Ji's approach is persistent resistance against injustice, utilising moral force rather than physical power, mainly when someone more powerful is unwilling to adopt the just path.

The boys exchanged glances; the concept was still nebulous in their young minds.

"Like when *Bhaiya* refused to eat last week until Mother gave him his favourite sweet?" Chinmay asked, referring to their elder brother's occasional hunger strikes. Sometimes, *Dadda* (father) termed it Satyagraha in lighter moments.

Mohan laughed. It's more like that, but it differs in purpose," he paused, searching for a better example they might grasp. Satyagraha is a form of nonviolent protest for seeking something rightfully, much like a child crying for milk until the mother responds by feeding them.

"And it worked anywhere in society?" Ramveer asked, his eyes wide.

Both children were astonished—was the same stubborn insistence they used to persuade their parents, the very force with which Gandhi compelled the mighty British to yield to his will?

"It did," Mohan confirmed. Gandhi ji says that if your cause is just and your heart is pure, peaceful resistance is more potent than any sword.

Ramveer mulled this over, his expression thoughtful. "So, even the weak can stand against the powerful if they stand for what is right?"

"Exactly," Mohan said, ruffling the younger brother's hair without thinking—a gesture of affection he would never have considered a year earlier. However, it requires immense courage and discipline.

"I understand now," Ramveer said quietly, standing away from both brothers. Neither of the brothers could have guessed how deeply those words had planted themselves in his consciousness, seeds awaiting the right season to flourish.

Janki Devi, Chinmay's mother, observed this association with growing concern. Her maternal instincts were feared for this unusual association because they were deeply ingrained in her beliefs about ritual purity and social propriety. However, she occasionally supported them financially and generously used articles for the Tulsa family. She noticed that Ramveer now wore Chinmay's outgrown clothes, donning them with pride.

Each morning, Chinmay would depart for school with his elder siblings, returning with new knowledge and experiences in the afternoon. After school, he would slip away to meet Ramveer, bringing along all his books for homework and revision. Chinmay found great satisfaction in teaching and sharing with Ramveer what he had learned, which gave him a sense of psychological fulfilment. Their association evolved over the almost two and half year into a deeper bond—one child teaching out of the joy of sharing, while the other learned with a hunger for knowledge. It was driven purely by curiosity and a quest for understanding.

"Why can't you just ask your father for permission to join my school?" Chinmay asked one day about the simplicity of childhood, seeing no obstacle that adult determination couldn't overcome. We will enjoy the lessons together in class.

That evening, Ramveer expressed his interest in formal education to his parents—the first time they were forced to confront the harsh reality of their social position with their curious child. His two elder sisters helped their mother with domestic work for upper-caste homes, continuing the cycle that had entrapped their ancestors for centuries. Not a single child from their community had ever attended the school, and no adult had even a simple understanding of reading.

"The school is not for people like us," his father, Budhai, explained gently, his calloused hands resting heavily on his son's shoulders. " Our work as *Dalits* is toil and labour, while education and learning belong to the upper castes."

"But why?" Ramveer asked the innocent question.

"Because we are not supposed to study but serve others, as we are *Dalits*; moreover, we don't have the intellect to read and write," Tulsa interjected, her voice soft but firm.

I am familiar with many poems, alphabets, and number tables, and I can read, write, and even recite them. If this is a requirement, I can demonstrate my ability to meet it for admission.

Surprised, as they had seen a miracle, Budhai and Tulsa exchanged startled glances, recognising in their son's question the spark of ambition they had wished for from the Almighty many times in their agony.

"Where did you learn all this?" Budhai exclaimed.

"From the books Chinmay shared with me every afternoon in the orchard, behind the mango tree, when everyone was busy with routine work," Ramveer answered truthfully.

But in her embrace, Tulsa felt something had fundamentally changed in her son—a new stillness, a resolve forming in his young mind that frightened and secretly thrilled her.

Ultimately, the parents pacified the little child for the moment by promising to speak with the school.

Days passed, and Budhai and Tulsa still showed no sign of fulfilling their promises, as they had little time for their kids.

Frustrated, the little champions resolved to bring the matter before *Dadda* (they call Shivraman with due respect).

One calm evening, Chinmay found his father in a delightful mood. Seeing an opportunity, he gathered his courage and asked the question that had been troubling him for a long time.

"*Dadda* (Father)," he began carefully, his voice steady yet hesitant, "why can't Ramveer, our housemaid's son, go to school like the rest of us?"

Shivraman looked annoyed and spoke casually, "It is not a matter of concern for you to be concerned about this; this is not your job; just focus on your studies."

"But you said that education is a right for every Indian child, as we are now independent," Chinmay countered in a fragmented lisping tongue, his young face serious. "You said that Dr. Ambedkar rose from being a *Dalit* to becoming one of India's most remarkable minds through education during a discussion with some guests."

Shivraman, surprised to hear these words from his little son, sighed and put down his pen. "What I believe personally and what is possible in Ratanpur are not always aligned, my son."

"Why not?" Chinmay persisted with curiosity. "You're the educated and respected man in the village. Who would oppose you if you say Ramveer should go to school?"

A bitter smile touched Shivraman's lips. "You overestimate my influence. All people in the school—teachers and students from upper-caste families—will object to the admission of a *Dalit* child," he explained. "I am not powerful enough to manage opposition from eleven villages. It would bring ruin upon us all."

In that case, what gain do we truly secure through its hard-won independence? Chinmay inquired, his tone edged with discontent.

Shivraman replied, then, seeing his son's crestfallen expression, added more gently and affectionately, "The Constituent Assembly—the body drafting India's constitution under Dr. Ambedkar's leadership—has resolved to guarantee education for all castes and communities." But the gap between Delhi's proclamations and village enforcement remains vast." However, you are too young to understand all this at your age.

Chinmay could not understand this; his young mind was not yet mature enough to grasp the complex interplay of what his father was discussing, encompassing difficult words that bridged idealism and pragmatism, moral certainty, and social reality.

He was annoyed and finally tried to understand his way.

"What would Gandhi ji do?" he asked innocently.

The question caught Shivraman off guard. "Gandhi ji?"

"Yes. " What would Mahatma Gandhi do if most of us followed this unfair rule?" the little boy asked.

Shivraman looked at his youngest son with new eyes, recognising in the child's question a moral clarity he was compromising in his daily life.

"Gandhi ji would likely suggest Satyagraha—peaceful resistance to unjust practices," he answered slowly.

"Thank you, Dadda," Chinmay said with unusual formality, bowing slightly before leaving the study.

Watching his son depart, Shivraman felt a curious mixture of pride and apprehension, unaware that he had just provided the spark to ignite a small revolution in Ratanpur.

The following morning, before the village had fully awakened, Chinmay took a water vessel and informed his *Amma* (mother), "I have stomach ache; going to the field to relieve myself" (It was usual practice in the society at that period)

"Chinmay went straight to Ramveer's house, where he was still fast asleep in his hut.

Calling out to him from outside, Chinmay woke him up.

Rubbing his eyes in surprise, Ramveer stepped outside, astonished. It was the first time in two years that Chinmay had come to his hut—and that too, so early in the day.

As Ramveer emerged, Chinmay spoke firmly, "We will undertake a Satyagraha until you are admitted to the school."

Ramveer gazed with puzzled eyes, struggling to understand.

"We're going to use Satyagraha to get you admitted to school," Chinmay repeated.

"Satyagraha?" Ramveer echoed, remembering their earlier discussions. "But how?"

"It's simple. You'll come to school with me today, and we'll sit peacefully outside the gate until they agree to let you in, " Chinmay explained.

"They'll never agree," Ramveer said, though his fingers traced the shirt's fabric with unconcealed longing.

"They might not at first," Chinmay acknowledged. But if we persist peacefully, they'll eventually have to listen. That's what Gandhi ji taught—if your cause is just and your heart is pure, peaceful resistance will prevail. After all, we are now independent."

"My parents will be terrified," Ramveer whispered. "Upper-caste men might burn our hut if I do this."

Chinmay, overwhelmed with emotion, exclaimed, 'So, did the British burn down Gandhi Ji's house?' After a moment's thought, he added, 'Perhaps they imprisoned him instead!' Well, if you are ever sent to jail, I will go with you. Together, we shall study there as well. Though he did not know much about imprisonment or 'jail. '

Ramveer saw something in his younger friend that transcended their childish games—determination and courage that came not only from privilege but from some unknown reasons.

"Tomorrow morning, then," Chinmay said, extending his hand for the first time in this almost two and half years of companionship.

Ramveer took it with hesitation—it was another small revolution in a village where such a touch across caste lines was taboo.

"Tomorrow," he agreed, his voice steadier than his racing heart.

The following dawn brought a perfect autumn morning—crisp air carrying the scent of ripening wheat, the sky an impossible blue unmarred by clouds. At the gates of Ratanpur High School, two tiny figures seated themselves in the dust, backs straight, faces composed in expressions of peaceful determination.

Chinmay wore his proper school uniform, and his books were neatly arranged beside him. Ramveer, wearing Chinmay's outgrown clothes, which were carefully washed but had many wrinkles, sat cross-legged a little away from his friend.

The first to notice them was the school peon, who stared in confusion before hurrying inside to inform the headmaster. Soon, a small crowd gathered—teachers arriving for the day's lessons, students trickling in with curious glances, and parents lingering to witness the unprecedented sight.

The headmaster, a portly Vidyanath who took pride in his orthodoxy, approached with a thunderous expression.

"What is the meaning of this?" he demanded, addressing Chinmay while ignoring Ramveer pointedly. "Why are you sitting outside instead of joining the assembly?"

"We are practising Satyagraha, sir," Chinmay replied politely but firmly. Ramveer wishes to attend school, and I support him for admission.

"Nonsense!" spluttered the headmaster. There has never been a *Dalit* student in this school, and there never will be as long as I am headmaster. Now come inside before I call your father.

"With respect, sir, I cannot abandon my colleague as Gandhi Ji always supported the downtrodden," Chinmay answered, his voice remarkably steady for a nine-year-old confronting authority. "We will remain here until Ramveer is admitted."

The playful antics of these children sparked curiosity among onlookers. Within no time, the news spread through the village, and a small crowd gathered on the spot. This created an obstacle for the school staff in their attempts to end what had become the smallest Satyagraha in history, forcibly.

"By noon, the school was in uproar. Teachers threatened to resign, and parents arrived to withdraw their children, claiming their sons would be polluted by sitting in the same classroom with untouchable. Through it all, the two boys remained seated, neither engaging in arguments nor responding to provocations—a lesson in Satyagraha more potent than any academic lecture could be.

News spread quickly, reaching Shivraman at his home. He rushed to the school, both angry at his son's disobedience and secretly proud of his moral courage. Arriving to find a crowd surrounding the boys, some jeering, others merely watching in shock, Shivraman pushed through to stand before his son.

"Chinmay," he said, his voice controlled despite his inner turmoil, "you just need to come home with me now."

Chinmay looked up at his father, respect in his eyes, speaking in a wavering but resolute voice. "I cannot, *Dadda*. Not until the school allow admission."

"This is not a game," Shivraman hissed, mindful of the watching crowd. You're causing a disruption that could have severe consequences.

Isn't that what Mahatma Gandhi did for all of us? Chinmay asked innocently in a lisping tongue.

Shivraman found himself speechless, hoisted by his own intellectual petard. He had raised his son on stories of freedom fighters and social reformers, never expecting the child to apply those lessons so directly—and inconveniently.

"Go home, Ramveer," he said finally. You are too young; "we will discuss this and outline some provisions."

Ramveer, who had remained silent throughout this exchange, finally spoke. "*Dadda* (the respectful term for upper-caste elders)," he said, addressing Shivraman with appropriate deference in his childish tongue," if Chinmay goes home, I will continue alone."

The simple dignity of this statement, coming from a child society deemed untouchable, silenced the murmuring crowd. Shivraman looked at Ramveer—looked at him, perhaps for the first time—and saw a boy of uncommon courage.

"I believe this matter deserves more discussion," Shivraman suggested, turning to the nearby headmaster. "Could we arrange a meeting with the school committee?"

"There is nothing further to discuss!"Vidyanath declared with a firm edge to his voice. Specific rules and regulations govern our school, and beyond these, it becomes an insurmountable task to manage the parents of the students and the teachers.

"And India has a future," a voice rose calmly from the crowd. Young individuals from upper-caste backgrounds, who had begun attending social organizations, recognized the evolving sentiments within the political and social landscape. They advocated for inclusion with a sense of respect and understanding.

In the *Dalit* quarter of Ratanpur, opinions about this unprecedented incident were divided. Some admired the boy's courage with surprise for understanding and following the Gandhian way of resistance. In contrast, others criticised Budhai for allowing his son to jeopardise the fragile peace they maintained with the upper castes through submissiveness.

"Your son will bring ruin upon us all," warned an elderly man who had witnessed attempts at caste rebellion being crushed mercilessly in his youth.

"Perhaps," Budhai acknowledged, surprising himself with his calm. Or perhaps he will open a door that none of us dared approach.

By the evening, what had begun as a two boys' protest, people sharing casually as some creative play, had transformed into a Satyagraha led by the youngest Satyagrahi in history, evoking a controversy that created a deepening ideological divide beyond the caste line throughout the region.

Youths and modernists who had encountered progressive ideas through volunteer organizations questioned inherited prejudices, while traditionalists forecasted and sensed some natural calamity.

Finally, Shivraman played his final card—a letter from an official working in district administration under the district magistrate. The letter gently reminded the headmaster that, although the Constitution of India was still being drafted, its principles were already evident, and it prohibited discrimination based on caste in educational institutions. More pointedly, it suggested that schools refusing to comply with this new vision of India might face the loss of government aids in the years to come.

A special school committee meeting was convened in following days, and heated arguments continued late into the evening. In the end, pragmatism prevailed over prejudice—though by the narrowest of margins. It was only due to an unprecedented step taken by the two kids—unaware of the far-reaching consequences of their actions—that they perhaps became the youngest Satyagrahis of Gandhian philosophy.

This autumn, a miracle occurred in Ratanpur. Ramveer walked through the gates of the Higher Secondary School—

not through the back entrance, as some had suggested as a compromise —but through the main door, becoming the first *Dalit* child in the region to receive formal education. Beside him walked Chinmay, their shadows merging on the dusty path as they stepped together into a future neither could fully envision but both would profoundly shape.

This was not a victory celebration but the beginning of new challenges. Immediate sanctions were imposed on Ramveer: he could not drink water from the common pots, he needed to be careful as he was not allowed to touch anyone, his homework had to be shown from a little distance, and he was relegated to a corner to save students from his defiled body. Their parents forbade other students from speaking with him or sharing items with him.

CULTURAL & CONTEXTUAL GLOSSARY:

Dadda: A term used respectfully for 'Father' and, often, by younger people for elders in the northern part of India.

Amma: A term used for 'Mother' and, often, by younger people for elder women in respect across the Indian subcontinent.

Bhaiya: A term of respect used for an elder brother in the northern states of India.

Achhoot: A term historically used in India to refer to the 'untouchable' castes, now replaced by the term *Dalit* to assert dignity and identity.

CHAPTER III

Lessons Beyond Textbooks: The Struggle for Dignity

The classroom fell silent as Ramveer entered, with every young face turning to stare at the unprecedented intruder in their midst. The class itself seemed to hold its breath—the usual shuffling and whispered conversations were suspended in a moment of collective shock.

Master Harish Chandra, the mathematics teacher, stood at the blackboard. His face betrayed nothing, but his knuckles whitened around the chalk. "Take your seat," he finally indicated towards an isolated space far from the group, his voice neutral yet carrying an undercurrent of tension that every child felt.

The class was under a temporary thatched shade on wooden pillars, open from all sides. The only space was at the back, near the trunk of a neem tree that overshadowed this thatched area. Ramveer moved toward it with measured steps, conscious of each pair of eyes following his progress. The boy to his left edged away fractionally as he sat, even though there was sufficient space, indicating how most students welcomed this new unwanted guest.

Chinmay, seated near the front as befitted his status as a senior student and the zamindar's son, turned slightly, offering an encouraging nod. Ramveer straightened his shoulders, opened his borrowed old textbook, and thus began his formal education. A cluster of children of various grades, comprising different age groups, sat on small pieces of jute, echoing the words spoken by their teacher. It was a fitting scene for today's youth to understand the ancient Gurukul education system — a time when paper had not yet been invented.

The incident had become a matter of intense discussion throughout the region. From a sociological perspective, society was divided into three groups beyond caste lineage.

The first group consisted of staunch traditionalists, who viewed the event as a harbinger of impending catastrophe. To them, it was a direct assault on the delicate social fabric woven over centuries. Many believed such incidents were signs of *Kaliyuga*—the dark age foretold in Hindu scriptures—when divine intervention would be required to restore order on earth. Notably, this sentiment was not exclusive to the upper caste; even a few of the so-called *Dalits (known as untouchables)* and other backwards communities shared these concerns.

The second group consisted of those who had witnessed and accepted the winds of social change. Their encounters with modern ideas, through various social movements and reformist organisations, gradually reshaped their thinking. They embraced these new ideals, recognizing that society was transforming progressively.

The third group was somewhere in between. They valued tradition yet were cautiously receptive to change. Like skilled meteorologists, they could sense the shifting currents of society and knew how to present their views diplomatically before the staunch, powerful traditionalists, very cleverly aligning their opinions and body language according to the position of the discussion, thereby securing a side that held the upper hand.

It was Dussehra, a grand festival in the village. The air was thick with the sweet aroma of freshly made delicacies. Children wore new dresses, adults wore traditional outfits, and women busied themselves in their kitchens. Laughter and excitement filled the streets.

Among the many customs observed, the *Vaishya* (trader) families upheld a long-standing tradition—they would offer *paan* (betel leaves) to their guests in the evening and distribute sweets to children. The act of sharing *paan* was not just a social gesture; it was an invitation to conversations that stretched deep into the night, where people of all castes and classes engaged in lively discussions.

Pandit Ramakant, the village priest, stepped into the bustling festival streets. As tradition dictated, he encountered Shivraman, a respected but unconventional figure in the community. They exchanged warm greetings, and Shivraman, in keeping with custom, offered the priest a neatly folded Bida—a betel leaf filled with dry nuts for chewing—before bowing to touch his feet, a gesture of reverence.

But Pandit Ramakant suddenly turned to the gathering crowd and, in a sharp, mocking tone, declared, "There is no meaning left in these traditions anymore. It's time to abandon them! You, Shivraman, have turned them into a mere mockery!"

Shivraman, unshaken, responded with quiet composure, "Panditji, let us continue to uphold the traditions we were raised with. At the same time, let the new generations create even better ones.

Before Ramakant could reply, Thakur Vijay Chandra, a man of Kshatriya lineage, interjected with disdain, "So, you mean to say that our children will no longer follow our traditions? This may be the case in your family or your caste, Shivraman, but in our higher lineage, such possibilities are unthinkable!

Shivraman, though deeply unsettled by the words, composed himself. Then, with piercing simplicity, he asked, "Panditji, tell me—what was Lord Ram's lineage?"

A voice from the crowd answered, *"Suryavanshi Kshatriya!"*

Shivraman nodded and continued, "And what about Lord Krishna?"

Again, a voice responded, *"Yaduvanshi!"*

Pandit Ramakant did not attempt to respond, as these questions seemed quite basic to him; anyone could answer them.

Now, with unshakable resolve, Shivraman declared,

If even the gods themselves have changed traditions over time—if *Lord Rama* was born into a noble and higher lineage and *Lord Krishna* into a lesser one, a lower lineage, both are incarnations of *Lord Vishnu*—then why do we, the followers, hold on so rigidly to these outdated beliefs?

A murmur spread through the gathering. Then, one of the 'moderates' in the crowd—the so-called meteorologists of society—spoke up, "We are all ignorant in such matters. Surely, Panditji can best answer this question."

Pandit Ramakant was unprepared for this dramatic turn. Seeing the crowd watch him with amusement, he hesitated. His authority, long unquestioned, now wavered under their scrutinising gaze. In embarrassment, he made a hurried attempt to leave.

Before he could step away, Shivraman's voice rang out, now more assertive than before, "Panditji, I have one final question before you leave—if God were born into a *Dalit* family this time, would you be willing to worship and respect Him?"

The question hung in the air, heavy and unanswerable. The festival's cheer had momentarily quieted, replaced by the weight of an idea too powerful to ignore.

The first few months were a time of profound isolation in the class. Ramveer's questions went unanswered during lessons, and his answers, when he dared to provide them, received only cursory responses. At recess, he sat alone beneath the neem tree, watching other children play games from which he was silently excluded. Papers he had touched were handled with hesitation; water he had been near was deemed impure or contaminated.

Yet through it all, Ramveer persisted with a quiet dignity that gradually earned, if not acceptance, then grudging recognition of his right to be there. His academic performance was unimpeachable—his memory was prodigious, his reasoning clear, and his writing advanced beyond his years, thanks to Chinmay's earlier tutelage.

He joined school nearly two and half years later than his peers, yet within a few months, he had mastered the entire syllabus. His secret? He spent afternoons quietly in the orchard with Chinmay, absorbing lessons far from the watchful eyes of the village elders.

When his abilities were revealed, the entire school was astonished. He made the other students seem sluggish by comparison. "Even the teachers, though reluctant to acknowledge it, were forced to admit that his pace of learning was almost unnatural—an enigma they could neither explain nor ignore."

It was Chinmay who unknowingly built the bridge between Ramveer and the insular world of the school. In public, Chinmay conformed to the traditions expected of him, never questioning the rigid social structures that governed their village. Yet, beneath this façade, his intellectual curiosity and subconscious superiority complex drove him to teach, discuss, and correct Ramveer's reading and writing—often after school, under the shade of the old mango tree. For Chinmay, it was an academic alliance rather than an act of social defiance.

He sometimes offered Ramveer a few sweets or other small necessities, which he would take only with his mother's permission. These gestures, though seemingly insignificant, created a quiet bond between them—one that went unnoticed by the larger community.

Until this point, their association was carefully distanced within the confines of the orchard. They neither arrived together nor returned home at the same time. Chinmay walked with his elder siblings and the other boys of his caste, while Ramveer either lagged or strode ahead, alone. This separation ensured that society remained oblivious to the intellectual camaraderie they shared.

In a world that seldom looked beyond lineage, Chinmay saw in Ramveer more than just a student; he found a kindred spirit. While many classmates regarded books as mere burdens, Ramveer eagerly absorbed knowledge, mirroring Chinmay's passion. Their secret study sessions became the highlight of their days. Chinmay simply explained complex concepts, and Ramveer, with an enthusiasm that amazed his mentor, grasped them effortlessly.

Yet, beneath this shared pursuit of learning, unspoken currents ran deep. For Chinmay, there was a subtle pleasure in being needed, in being the one who held knowledge and had the power to share it. It nourished an ego he barely recognised within himself. For Ramveer, there was deep and sincere gratitude and the growing realisation that his education was not an entitlement but an act of charity. His place in this world depended not only on his merit but also on the benevolence of another.

Their academic rivalry grew sharper as the years passed, even as their friendship deepened. Ramveer displayed a natural aptitude in mathematics that sometimes outpaced Chinmay's more methodical approach. They debated interpretations in literature so intensely that even their teachers were left bemused. Their competition propelled them both forward.

In primary education, no rules prevented students from advancing to the next grade unless they had passed the lower-grade examinations. For the fifth-grade exams, it was at the principal's discretion to determine who should be allowed to take the examination.

Ramveer and Chinmay completed the syllabus up to fifth grade in nearly two years. With the support of the school staff, both received approval from the principal to sit for the fifth-grade examination. Not only did they pass, but they also secured the highest marks in the entire school. Chinmay, in particular, achieved a historic feat by obtaining the highest marks ever recorded in the school's history for the fifth standard.

This leads to a reputation for both, not only in their village but also in other villages in the region. Both are working continuously for the junior classes and are approaching the most awaited exam, a truly significant milestone in their area, an achievement that very few have ever reached. For Ramveer, it was more than just an exam; it was a battle against the doubts and dismissals of many.

Peers, teachers, and village elders frequently taunted him, saying, "It's not easy to pass this exam." Let's see where you stand once it's over."

It was the first time a Dalit child in the entire region appeared for the high school board examination.

Inside the exam hall, boys hunched over their papers, pens moving with the confidence of the well-prepared. When the final bell rang, the weight of expectation settled heavily on Ramveer's shoulders.

After the exams, the two boys met at their usual spot beneath the mango tree. They discussed their answers, cross-checked responses, and recounted lessons they had overheard at home. Unlike the scepticism of their doubters, they felt no uncertainty—both knew their results would be nearly identical. In the days that followed, Chinmay even borrowed books from his elder siblings, and together, they began studying the next level of coursework, slowly but steadily.

When the results were posted on the school notice board after almost two months, a crowd gathered in hushed astonishment. The boys' academic prowess was undeniable. Chinmay had ranked first in the district, which filled the onlookers with pride. Ramveer, just four points behind, secured second place, a testament to their hard work and dedication.

That evening, Shivraman, Chinmay's father, hosted a modest celebration at home. He distributed sweets, beaming with pride, not just for his son's achievement but for his foresight in supporting Chinmay's academic endeavours. For years, his family had failed to understand his vision, but today, his youngest child had proven him right.

As Shivraman handed Ramveer a sweet, his voice carried more weight than mere congratulations. "Your success brings honour to yourself and your entire community," he said. Do you understand what that means?"

Ramveer nodded, feeling the invisible burden that had settled on his young shoulders. I must succeed not just for myself but for all those like me who may follow.

Shivraman regarded him thoughtfully. "Yes," he said. "But remember—your duty is not just to be a symbol. Live for yourself, too. The struggle for justice is not won by becoming an icon alone, but by embracing your full humanity, with all its complexities."

That night, as Ramveer walked home with his parents, the sky above seemed closer, the stars hanging lower as if listening to his thoughts. Behind him lay childhood innocence; ahead stretched the uncharted possibilities that education had unlocked. And though Chinmay was not by his side then, his presence lingered— an invisible companion woven into every step of the path that now lay open before him.

Haunted by this thought, Ramveer remained lost in contemplation, but his parents grappled with a new dilemma. How would they afford his books and clothing for higher studies? Their finances were strained after their daughter's marriage, and a high-interest loan loomed over them. They had quietly hoped Ramveer would begin working after this examination and contribute to repaying the debt. However, their expectations crumbled after overhearing the discussions at Shivraman's home about his further education after his grand success.

Budhai and Tulsa had a serious concern and decided to share it with Shivraman. He had been passively supporting their child on this uncommon path. But how could they ask for more when he had already helped them significantly during the marriages of Savitri and Meera?

By the following morning, several activists had begun visiting Budhai's small, remote hut. Everyone was praising his decision to allow his child to pursue education, even those traditionalists within his community who had once predicted calamity due to Ramveer's admission to school, now offered their hesitant congratulations.

Amidst the gathering and discussions, someone suddenly announced that Ramveer was entitled to the *Wajeefa*, a government scholarship for Dalit students pursuing higher education. This unexpected news lifted a significant burden from Budhai and Tulsa, who, for the first time, felt a profound sense of pride in their son's success.

Overwhelmed with relief, Budhai eagerly inquired about the amount *Wajeefa,* Ramveer would receive. This stranger replied that it would be somewhere between fifty to eighty rupees per month.

It was a great relief for Budhai, as this amount was more than sufficient for his son. With gratitude welling up in his heart, Budhai offered a silent prayer to the Almighty and then called Ramveer over, urging him to find out how to apply for the *Wajeefa* from that stranger.

Later that night, in his hut, a lingering question troubled Ramveer's mind—one that his simple yet inquisitive nature could not ignore: 'If the upper-caste people in his village and school had always tried to block his education, then why do influential leaders and officials genuinely care about uplifting *Dalits*? They made laws, offered scholarships, and spoke of change—but what benefits do they have for the poor like us in return?'

Amidst his deep, innocent thoughts, Ramveer resolved that one day he would seek an answer from *Dadda*, a term of respect used by those in his community for Shivraman.

Chinmay and Ramveer gradually noticed a shift in behaviour among the elders from the upper caste. They had treated Ramveer harshly, but now displayed a particular kindness toward him—an acknowledgement of his academic achievements. Yet, beneath this surface respect, the ingrained prejudice against Dalits had not entirely faded. However, the villagers had at least begun to accept Chinmay and Ramveer's companionship with a positive mindset, which was no small achievement for Ramveer.

Chinmay and Ramveer were admitted to a Intermediate college in a nearby town, nearly fifteen kilometres from their village—a journey marked by a narrow, winding path often broken by meandering streams, as if nature itself tested their resolve with every step. While this was a step forward in their academic journey, it also laid bare the stark realities of systemic exclusion. Like many institutions of the time, the college lacked hostel accommodations for *Dalit* students, creating yet another barrier to their education.

For Ramveer, securing admission was only part of the struggle. Despite earning a government scholarship, known as *Wazeefa*, he faced an insurmountable challenge—there was simply no place for him in the hostel. The institution had neither allocated space for *Dalit* students nor made provisions for segregated housing, a grim reflection of the deeply entrenched caste hierarchies that extended beyond classrooms into every aspect of daily life.

Determined to find a way forward, Chinmay and Ramveer devised an unconventional solution. After much persuasion, they convinced the hostel warden to register Ramveer as a resident, at least on paper. This allowed him to claim his scholarship and access hostel facilities. He would continue living in the nearby *Dalit Basti*, a segregated settlement on the outskirts of town.

The arrangement, though far from ideal, gave them a critical advantage. With their academic futures intertwined, the two friends now had more opportunities to study together on campus after classes, strengthening their bond in the face of adversity.

As they navigated this deeply flawed system, their friendship became a quiet rebellion—an unspoken defiance against the rigid social order that sought to keep them apart.

During the summer vacation, they dedicated long hours to studying under the shade of the mango orchards, which had become their sanctuary of learning. Their relentless preparation bore fruit—when classes resumed, they answered their teachers' questions with remarkable ease and posed deeply thought-provoking queries that impressed their instructors.

When institutional support and personal commitment converge, success is amplified manifold. This was precisely what happened with Chinmay and Ramveer. They excelled in higher secondary examinations and secured top ranks in their district and the state board's ranking list. With this achievement, both friends began receiving scholarships, and the invisible social barriers that had once divided them started to dissolve. After completing higher secondary education, they pursued further studies at Allahabad University, an institution renowned for its intellectual excellence.

Cultural & Contextual Glossary:

Wazeefa: A scholarship or financial aid granted to meritorious students, particularly those from marginalised communities.

Kaliyuga: It is the last of the four great ages in Hindu Traditional scriptures, often described as an era of moral decline and chaos.

Vaishya: The merchant and trading caste in the Hindu varna system.

Paan (Bida): Betel leaves, often chewed with areca nut and spices, are traditionally offered as a sign of hospitality and social bonding.

Suryavanshi & Yaduvanshi: Lineages in Hindu mythology. Lord Ram belonged to the Suryavanshi (Solar) dynasty, while Lord Krishna belonged to the Yaduvanshi (Yadu) clan, illustrating that divinity transcended social hierarchies.

Dalit Basti: A settlement where Dalit families traditionally reside, often on the periphery of villages or towns due to historical caste segregation.

Thatched: A Shade made of long sticks of agricultural waste.

Dussehra: A significant Hindu festival celebrated across India. It commemorates the victory of good over evil, specifically the triumph of Lord Rama over the demon king Ravana.

Lord Vishnu: A principal deity in Hinduism, is primarily known as the preserver and protector of the universe.

Lord Ram: Lord Vishnu's incarnation was born in King Bharat's Suryavansi clan to demonstrate the most dignified way of life.

Lord Krishna: Lord Vishnu's incarnation took birth to demonstrate the importance of dharma (duty) with dedication and letting go of attachment to the results.

CHAPTER IV

Breaking Boundaries: A Journey of Transformation

Allahabad opened up like a vibrant dream. In this city, history etched its lasting presence on grand structures, where spirituality fused with contemporary institutions of rationality, literature, and culture in Hindi, English, and Urdu. The polite rhythm of its dialogue and the intriguing blend of modernity with tradition enchanted their senses. For the two boys from Ratanpur, this city symbolised more than just advanced education; it was a gateway to an extensive world of ideas and opportunities.

The campus of Allahabad University stands as a legacy of academic excellence in the city's heart. Its historic buildings, influenced by *Indo-Saracenic* architecture, reflect a fusion of tradition and modernity. As Ramveer and Chinmay stepped through the main gate for the first time, the autumn sun casting a golden hue over the iconic clock tower, they felt a profound sense of history and ambition intertwining, marking the beginning of their journey at this prestigious institution.

"It seems as if we have entered a different country," Ramveer murmured. His eyes widened as he took in the cosmopolitan hustle of students from diverse backgrounds weaving their way purposefully between the buildings.

"Not a separate realm, but a radiant part of our nation," Chinmay responded, with a tone both steady and optimistic. "This is the India we've envisioned—a place where tradition and transformation harmoniously coexist."

Their dormitory was modest but sufficient—two narrow beds, two wooden desks, a shared bookshelf, and a window overlooking a courtyard where ancient trees cast dappled shadows on groups of students engaged in animated discussions. Here, amid young men drawn from across the state and beyond, they dared to hope that the rigid caste distinctions of their village might finally loosen their grip. Although the university's education system formally has no discrimination based on caste and creed, its social fabric was woven with invisible yet potent fault lines. Certain study groups remained exclusively upper-caste, and particular tables in the dining hall were tacitly reserved for Brahmins. Subtle nuances in speech and behaviour marked students' backgrounds as unmistakably as any formal label.

Sensing this division, the youth from Ratanpur usually spent most of their time together reading, writing, and discussing. However, they decided to take separate rooms, following the traditional cultural patterns of their village, which was attuned to the university's cultural system beyond formal education.

Stepping into the university's cross-cultural environment, Ramveer experienced a stark cultural shift from the explicit casteism he had grown up witnessing in his village and school. On the surface, the new climate seemed more progressive— people seemed measured in their words, conscious of appearing inclusive. Yet beneath this civility lay a more insidious form of discrimination.

He quickly found himself navigating a complex web of unspoken biases. Professors who praised his academic brilliance would, without realising it, recoil ever so slightly when handing back his graded papers. Classmates engaged him enthusiastically in heated debates over philosophy and politics, but conveniently excluded him from casual tea breaks and social outings. Even the hostel staff seemed unusually meticulous, which is evident in the difference in the quality of services in his room compared to those of the upper castes.

This was a different kind of marginalisation—polished and disguised under the veneer of modernity, yet rooted in centuries of social conditioning. While the chains of caste were no longer always visible, their weight still lingered in the silence, in the sideways glances, and in the unspoken exclusions.

Yet, amid these trials, rays of hope emerged—small but meaningful shifts that hinted at the possibility of a more equitable future. Professor Mehta, who taught political philosophy, recognised the sharp clarity of Ramveer's arguments and the depth of his understanding of constitutional values. He encouraged, opening a door that had long remained closed to people from a destitute background.

Chinmay remained Ramveer's steadfast ally, though the nature of their relationship had subtly evolved. No longer was Chinmay merely a benefactor with Ramveer as the grateful recipient; their intellectual exchange had grown into a dialogue of equals, each challenging the other's assumptions and broadening their horizons. Yet, the unspoken shadow of their disparate social origins lingered between them, evident in the dining hall and the sharing of simple meals.

University life was renowned for debates, which were not merely exchanges of words—they were vibrant contests of ideas that echoed through centuries of cultural legacy. Throughout their undergraduate years, the duo frequently attended gatherings, lectures, and intellectual debates organised by various social organisations. These institutions, which emerged during the Indian Renaissance, successfully eradicated numerous social evils such as the practice of Sati, child marriage, and the ban on widow remarriage. Moreover, by embracing the spirit of nationalism born out of political and social awakening, they kindled the flame of patriotism in the hearts of the youth.

These organisations resonated with both young men, transcending the discriminatory practices that had marred their early lives. The inclusive ethos of these groups, combined with their progressive visions of nationalism, inspired Ramveer to envision a society where caste divisions were relics of the past. For Ramveer, these meetings were sanctuaries of hope—a renewed call to contribute meaningfully to a nation built on an inclusive social framework.

These institutions undoubtedly accorded due respect to all great personalities, regardless of caste, religion, or gender, who had valiantly fought against foreign invaders or battled entrenched social evils to awaken a dormant societal conscience. Yet, this admiration was primarily confined to discussions, lectures, and formal debates on their work and teachings.

These historical figures were celebrated and honoured like heroes in daily life, but their luminous paths were seldom trodden by those who acclaimed them. Many scholars who vociferously denounced the rigid caste system born of the ancient Varna hierarchy found themselves paradoxically compelled to adhere to the same social stratification in their personal lives.

It was similar to Pandit Ramakant's unwavering devotion to sacred scriptures—he would recite and cherish them. Still, he could not tolerate any form of discussion or critical analysis about these, particularly from any other caste group. This glaring contradiction was not an aberration of our society alone. History had shown, through episodes like the Church's persecution of Galileo, who posited that the Sun, not the Earth, is at the centre. It clearly shows that across the planet, organisations harbour an institutional ego—a refined and magnified collective of individual ego that suppresses innovation and critical thinking.

Midway through the session, an incident arose in their final year of graduation, leading to a rift in their association like never before. During an informal group discussion in a hostel room, heated debates broke out over the reservation system—policies that reserve seats in government jobs and educational institutions for Scheduled Castes and Scheduled Tribes. The room was packed, buzzing with the electric energy of passionate debate. Students sat cross-legged on floor cushions or perched on window sills, notebooks open, expressions intent. Chinmay sat near the front, his face alight with pride.

Amid this discussion, Vikram Singh, a student from a poor *Kshatriya* family known for his traditional views, drawled, "Reservation in educational institutions, financial assistance, and even in representation can be justified under various constitutional provisions intended for social justice, and at the same time, the framework established by Articles 309, 16, 14, and 320 indicates that recruitment into public services should be based solely on merit."

Suddenly, Kanhaiya—a final-year law student—interjected, "Yet the same Constitution provides for reservations for Scheduled Castes and Scheduled Tribes who have been inadequately represented under Articles 330 and 332."

"What a dichotomy—mockery of merit!" Vikram and Kanhaiya erupted simultaneously.

Chinmay asked politely, "Did you finish your point? The Constitution doesn't just aim for legal equality," he continued, glancing around the room. "It seeks to create a balance between regions, communities, castes, and interests through mechanisms such as affirmative action. However, that balance only makes sense when we stop seeing ourselves merely as 'upper' or 'lower' castes and instead start thinking of ourselves as citizens of an inclusive society."

He paused briefly, then added, more softly, "Are we genuinely ready to internalise the fundamental constitutional values? Despite Article 17 and decades of efforts by various socio-cultural institutions, have we succeeded in eradicating untouchability? Even I, on a personal note, have not shared a meal with Ramveer in the fifteen years of our close association."

He looked up, locking eyes with the group. "Now, tell me honestly—could we have competed fairly with a British candidate in a colonial-era English exam with just a small financial aid? Wouldn't we have needed the same ecosystem of learning, mentoring, language, and social support they had?"

Kanhaiya leaned forward, unwilling to let it pass. "Yes, many Indians competed with the British during the colonial era— Subhash Chandra Bose, Satyendra Nath Tagore, and Behari Lal Gupta are a few examples who cracked the civil services during more challenging times. They proved that merit could rise despite discrimination."

Chinmay smiled faintly, then said, almost challengingly, "Then I would like invite you, all, to spend just a few weeks in a Dalit Basti—not as a visitor, but as one among them. Try navigating daily life through your lens—the daily struggle for school, healthcare, and even access to food and water. And then, let me know: is the discrimination faced by zamindars under British rule, who succeed in examinations in an open competition, truly the same as the everyday humiliation Dalits still face from their fellow Indians?"

Ramveer carefully tried to understand the opinions being expressed. No upper-class person had openly discussed this matter with him, as most considered it controversial. Moreover, this had been discussed many times with the students of his community, so he was aware of one side's ideology on this complicated issue.

During the heated discussion, Ramveer finally spoke after much contemplation, "Since its independence, India has held elections based on universal adult franchise; however, the Parliament remains dominated by upper-caste representatives. Despite this, laws have been enacted to uplift tribal and Dalit communities—a fact that continually astonishes me."

Pausing to gauge the room's reaction, he continued, "For years, I've struggled with this puzzle, but now I see it as a deliberate, albeit temporary, corrective measure to address centuries of exploitation and exclusion. These provisions are not permanent; they are meant to be re-evaluated and reformed by future parliaments to achieve equality among various social groups and simultaneously within the social groups. Otherwise, another privileged caste will soon emerge among the Scheduled Castes and Tribes—enjoying the rights of equality while still drawing from the reservations intended for the most oppressed."

A murmur of discussion rippled through the room until Vikram Singh cut sharply, "What a justification? And how convenient it is that you frame it that way. Of course, the 'damad'—a disparaging term implying one parasitically sustained by state benevolence—would defend a system that guarantees his position regardless of merit."

Ramveer's face remained impassive, though a muscle in his jaw twitched. "I have presented historical facts and constitutional principles based on judicious reasoning," he replied evenly. "If you have counterarguments, I welcome them. Personal insinuations add nothing to rational debate."

"Facts?" scoffed Vikram. "Here's a fact: without the quota and effective financial support, without the government carrying you across the threshold like a bride, you would still have been where nature intended—cleaning in some backwater village."

Except for Chinmay, the faces of nearly all the young attendees were devoid of expression. It seemed as though Vikram had earned their silent approval.

Chinmay began to rise, his face flushed with anger, but before he could speak, Ramveer's voice resonated through the charged silence. "Is that truly what you believe, Vikram? Facilities and environment do not determine intellectual capacity. It's a dangerous notion."

He continued with a steady voice, infused with conviction, 'Vikram, if you've reduced this intellectual discourse to a personal matter, let's make a bold personal commitment. From now on, you will not discriminate against any Dalit, not even in your village, at least on a personal account, and I renounce any entitlement to reservation benefits for employment. My future career will hinge solely on my merit. And if you're willing, let's start sharing meals together from now on.'

Laughter echoed in the room, casting a shadow over Vikram's face. Before he could respond, many participants began to clap for Ramveer.

A stunned silence followed. Chinmay's face shifted from pride to concern as he realised the seriousness of this declaration. Gradually, the conversation became hushed clusters as students tried to distance themselves from this controversy.

Later that evening, while they were discussing, Chinmay confronted Ramveer. "You should not possibly mean to follow through on this declaration. It was made in the heat of the moment."

Ramveer, gazing at the distant campus lights. "I meant every word," he replied softly.

"But reservations exist to help correct historical wrongs, as you also acknowledged!"

"Yes," Ramveer conceded, "and they have indeed served their purpose for me. Through them, I gained access to education and received resources that many *Dalits* never have. Continuing to claim special consideration now would deny my principles."

"Your principles?" Chinmay echoed, frustration lacing his tone. "Or is it simply ego?"

Ramveer turned to Chinmay, his expression both resolute and vulnerable. "Perhaps there is pride in my decision. Is that so terrible? Hasn't my dignity been assaulted enough that I wish to stand on equal footing, with no special pleading, just as any other man?"

Chinmay sat heavily on his bed, recognising in Ramveer's words not only determination but a subtle rebuke—a declaration of independence not just from the reservation system but also from my benevolent patronage.

"I cannot support this decision," Chinmay said, "but I must respect that it is your decision."

Outside, the ancient courtyard trees rustled in the night breeze, witnesses to countless student dramas over the years. Within Chinmay's room, the two young men faced each other across a gulf that had suddenly become visible—a gulf created not just by the accident of birth but by the interplay of privilege, gratitude, pride, and the universal longing for self-determination.

That night, Ramveer left in silence for his room, burdened by an agony that might keep him awake all night.

Cultural & Contextual Glossary:

Indo-Saracenic Architecture: A style that blends Indian architectural elements with Islamic and European influences, reflecting the cultural synthesis of colonial India.

Damad: A derogatory term implying a son-in-law who is perceived as overly dependent on state support or the benevolence of others.

Allahabad University: One of India's most prestigious universities, renowned for its history of producing intellectuals, political leaders, and academicians.

CHAPTER V

Betrayal or Renunciation

It was an ordinary day on the university campus when a notification published in an employment newspaper about recruitment for civil services by the Union Public Service Commission sparked a burst of energy among the final-year students. From the dormitories to tea stalls, classrooms to libraries, discussions buzzed with speculation and ambition. For decades, the All-India Services at the top of the civil service had represented the pinnacle of government service, with their officers wielding the power to shape the nation's policies and guide its development, even during political turmoil.

For Ramveer and Chinmay, this announcement crystallised long-held aspirations. Both had excelled academically, demonstrated leadership in campus activities, and honed the analytical skills demanded by the civil service. It was natural that they would both apply, yet the path ahead remained uncharted territory.

Within a few days, they had secured multi-page application forms—each brimming with exhaustive queries about personal background, scholastic achievements, and, most importantly, caste and education certificates sealed with the stamp of a gazetted officer. Over the next week, they hunted down every required document, made crisp photocopies of each, double-checked every line, and determined that nothing would stand between them and the opportunity they sought.

One afternoon, as they sat at their respective desks completing their forms after the lectures, Chinmay glanced over at Ramveer's application form and frowned.

"You've left the caste section blank, and the caste certificate also seems to be missing," he observed in a carefully neutral tone.

"Not blank," Ramveer corrected, not looking up from his work. I've checked the 'General Category'—as I vowed I would.

Chinmay set down his pen, troubled. "That was months ago, spoken in anger after Vikram's provocation. Surely, you've reconsidered?"

Ramveer's gaze finally met his friend's. I have given it careful consideration, and my decision remains unchanged.

This is an affront to the Constitution's vision and to the visionaries who have envisioned social justice through affirmative action. Chinmay played a new card.

"Rights which I am free to waive," Ramveer countered firmly. "The Constitution guarantees opportunity; it does not compel me to accept any advantage."

"It isn't about advantage—it's about correction, about justice," Chinmay argued, frustration edging his voice.

"Perhaps," Ramveer acknowledged softly, "but it feels like a form of continued dependence to me. I have already received support that most *Dalits* can only dream of—your family's patronage, university scholarships, and academic recognition. Continuing to claim special consideration now feels... unnecessary, as I have never yearned more than what I have achieved."

Chinmay presented his final argument: "In fact, the constitutional framework of the reservation system was created for people like you—those who have fought tirelessly to reach the threshold of this examination. Your defiance would seem much more rational if, after benefiting from the provisions of the reservation, the next generation chose to renounce it. This way, those in the *Dalit* community who remain deprived of this provision could benefit, thereby fortifying the very soul of the Constitution."

Their conversation spiralled into a heated debate, the tension in the room palpable. Each word revealed the tension that had long simmered between them—the unspoken expectation that Ramveer should conform to the ideals enshrined in the constitutional framework following a thorough debate in the constituent assembly, versus Ramveer's fierce desire to be judged solely by merit. Neither was willing to concede ground. Finally, they decided to stop the discussion on this.

As the application deadline approached, Ramveer finally submitted his completed application form to Chinmay. "Would you mind posting this with yours tomorrow? I promised Professor Mehta I'd help him organise his research materials, and I think I'll be occupied for the next few days."

Chinmay took the envelope, its weight representing years of study and ambition, and now, this was the ultimate point of contention between them. "Of course," he replied. I'll ensure it's delivered safely."

That night, Chinmay sat alone in his room. Before him lay the sealed envelope containing Ramveer's application; for the first time in their association, this document symbolised the divergent yet new view.

His thoughts churned like the sacred confluence of the Ganga and Yamuna at Sangam during the monsoon. Chinmay had always taken pride in his progressive ideals, unwavering commitment to equality, and rejection of caste-based prejudices. Yet, faced with Ramveer's bold decision to forgo reservation benefits in favour of an unmediated contest of merit, Chinmay wrestled with emotions he had long suppressed.

Was it genuine concern for Ramveer's welfare that troubled him? Or was it a more profound impulse—the need to preserve the subtle hierarchy that had always defined their relationship, where Chinmay was the guiding benefactor and Ramveer the grateful protégé?

Around midnight, Chinmay made his choice. He carefully steamed open the envelope with trembling hands, removed Ramveer's application, and made two critical alterations.

He just wrote "Yes" in the column for Scheduled Caste. He attached the caste certificate that Ramveer had used for the *Wazeefa* (scholarship) the previous year—a copy was already in Chinmay's documents. He meticulously resealed the envelope once the changes were complete, leaving no trace of his interference.

The following day, Chinmay posted both applications together, his face betraying nothing of the momentous betrayal he had just committed.

Chinmay believed he was safeguarding Ramveer's future by ensuring he benefited from the protections he deserved. The thought that this act might also preserve the moral superiority he had always claimed as the enlightened upper-caste ally was a justification he silently clung to.

Since childhood, Chinmay has assumed the role of guardian, while Ramveer followed him without question. Most of the time, his decisions resulted in tangible successes for both. Perhaps this dynamic was the foundation of their enduring association—a bond as rooted in dependency as in genuine friendship.

Yet, when Ramveer refused to fill out the reservation column on his application, it marked the first overt challenge to Chinmay's dominance. At that moment, Chinmay's quiet resolve gave way to an act of intervention he now deemed necessary for Ramveer's well-being. However, the psychological satisfaction he derived from this intervention was a bitter pill that underscored the complex interplay of privilege, duty, and personal ambition that had always defined their relationship.

Despite their differences of opinion on this particular personal issue, the two friends shared a deep alignment of thought on social issues. Therefore, beyond their bond, they never let their engagement and discussions on educational, social, and cultural matters falter.

Meetings and deliberations in Renaissance-era organisations became sanctuaries of hope for them—a call to contribute meaningfully to a nation envisioned as genuinely inclusive. In the vibrant lectures and impassioned discussions, they discovered role models transcending the narrow confines of caste, religion, and regional identity. The enduring messages of Kabir and the social justice advocacy of B.R. Ambedkar and Jyotiba Phule inspired them as guiding lights of justice and equality. At the same time, they marvelled at the valour and wisdom of historical warriors like Shivaji and Maharana Pratap, whose leadership redefined courage; and at the spiritual insights of Guru Nanak, Mahatma Buddha, and Adi Shankaracharya, whose teachings— rooted in ancient tradition yet resonant with universal truths— had shaped the cultural ethos of the land. These icons, emerging from every stratum of society, wove a rich tapestry of inspiration that fuelled Ramveer's ambition to redefine his destiny and contribute to a more equitable future. The inclusive ethos of these organisations, combined with their progressive visions of nationalism and the country's rich ancient history, inspired Ramveer to dream of a society where caste divisions would be relics of the past within the next few years, as he witnessed a gradual decline in discrimination throughout his educational journey.

Ramveer and Chinmay stood apart from the popular discourse that often-blamed foreign conquests for India's social ills—sati, child marriage, untouchability, and other deep-rooted injustices. They did not deny the impact of invasions or colonial rule, but they refused to accept these as the sole architects of India's centuries-long decline. In their view, the decay was homegrown—woven into the social fabric long before the first foreign invaders set foot on the land.

They believed the rot began from within. A rigid caste hierarchy had fractured the soul of the society, turning fellow citizens into strangers. Women, silenced and confined, were denied from decision making process. Talent was stifled beneath the burden of birth—occupations dictated by lineage, not ability; status determined by caste, not character. Such a system, they argued, did not merely suppress individuals—it suffocated the collective imagination of a civilisation.

To Ramveer and Chinmay, the repeated invasions India endured—from early medieval powers to colonial regimes— were not the causes of decay but its consequences. A society already weakened by internal division, moral stagnation, and institutionalized inequity had little strength left to resist external forces. The empire of the collective enterprise had crumbled before the empire of the sword could arrive.

In their reflections, the malaise was not confined to the past. Echoes of that ancient decay resounded in the present: in corruption masked as tradition, in systemic inequality disguised as culture, and in the enduring exploitation of the vulnerable. Whether it was the widow on a pyre or the girl denied education, the landlord hoarding wealth or the intellectuals justifying the occupation based on birth and lineage rather than merit—each, in their own way, was a reflection of an older, deeper rot.

While civilisations across the globe were visualising expansion through collective support, innovation and making strategies to occupy new territories most of India's ruling classes remained fixated on preserving the status quo. Kingdoms and social institutions, instead of embracing change, built walls around caste, privilege, and inherited power. The result was a brittle society, lacking the cohesive vision or adaptive energy necessary to withstand internal decay or external shocks. Without engines of economic renewal or structures of social mobility, the subcontinent became a patchwork of guarded hierarchies—rich in culture, yet poor in collective and inclusive progress.

CULTURAL & CONTEXTUAL GLOSSARY:

Indian Civil Services (ICS, now popularly known as All India Services): The highest echelon of government service in India, whose officers play a key role in formulating policies and steering national development. Which is now known as the Indian Administrative Services, including a range of All India Services and Central services

The Ramakrishna Mission is dedicated to spiritual and humanitarian work and is inspired by the teachings of Sri Ramakrishna.

Kabir: A 15th-century mystic poet and saint whose verses challenged established religious practices.

Shivaji & Maharana Pratap: Historical figures celebrated for their military prowess and leadership in resisting foreign domination.

Wajeefa: A term referring to a government-issued scholarship, particularly for marginalised communities such as Dalits, to support their educational pursuits.

Guru Nanak: the Founder of Sikhism, was a 15th-century spiritual leader who preached equality and social justice.

Mahatma Buddha: The founder of Buddhism, who renounced material life to seek enlightenment and preached against social hierarchies.

Varna system: The ancient Hindu caste hierarchy divides society into four main categories: Brahmins (priests), Kshatriyas (warriors), Vaishyas (merchants), and Shudras (labourers).

Ambedkar: Dr. B.R. Ambedkar was a social reformer, jurist, and the principal architect of the Indian Constitution who fought for the rights and equality of *Dalits*.

Sati Pratha: Prevalent practice in Indian subcontinent during Mughal and British rule in which a widow immolates herself on the funeral pyre of her deceased husband.

Purdah Pratha: A practice of seclusion and separation of women from public observation through a veil.

CHAPTER VI

Diverging Paths

The Union Public Service Commission has announced the examination dates, prompting round-the-clock preparation on university campuses. Ramveer and Chinmay—two friends often dubbed the "young Turks" for their reformist and intellectual zeal—resolved to immerse themselves entirely in their studies. The prestigious civil service examination conducted by the Union Public Service Commission required nothing less than the highest level of preparation, a straightforward thought process and logical understanding based on the fundamentals of various subject matter. When the admit cards finally arrived, each Admit card indicated the candidate's category—a detail that would soon prove fateful.

Ramveer enthusiastically checked his admit card. Suddenly, he was shocked as he had applied under the General category, his admit card inexplicably classified him as reserved under the Scheduled Caste category. Troubled by this anomaly, he sought Chinmay's counsel immediately.

Chinmay felt awkward—a brief moment of hesitation was followed by a measured expression of surprise that never quite reached his eyes. He suddenly checked again and said, "It might be a printing error," he suggested casually. We can write to the commission and request corrections. Trusting his friend implicitly, Ramveer set aside his misgivings for the time, as this was not the moment for writing anything for commission. They had been working on last year's examination papers and were now focused on completing them. The two resumed their intense, concentrated discussions on subjects vital to their upcoming examination.

When passion guides your work, time quietly slips away—as knowledge has no shoreline, and passion knows no stay. Finally, the examination approached. The duo took their papers with unwavering determination; their minds were clear on the subject matter and their lofty life vision.

The exam was rigorous, comprising papers from General Studies, language, and two elective subjects, followed by an essay paper, which took more than ten days to complete. Despite the challenges posed by the English medium and the rigorous test, they persevered and completed all their papers satisfactorily.

Following the exams, during the tranquil interlude between academic terms, an approaching festival prompted the friends to journey homeward. They boarded a train and found a peculiar last coach—a truncated general compartment divided into three distinct sections: the guard's cabin, a women's coach, and a general seating area that, though only one-third the capacity of a standard coach, fortunately had not much crowd amidst regular commuters and seasoned professionals.

At Kanpur station, the train took a little longer than usual. Suddenly, without warning, a contingent of police officers invaded the coach and imperiously ordered the immediate evacuation of all passengers. Within moments, most passengers dispersed into adjacent bogies. Yet Chinmay and Ramveer—spirited and inquisitive—stood their ground, asking the reason for this arbitrary order.

"The inspector on duty offered no satisfactory answer, brusquely stating that his team required the coach for their travel. But how many police officers are there?" Ramveer inquired calmly, gesturing toward the ample space that could easily accommodate officers and civilians.

Rather than understanding the advice, the inspector and his subordinates launched into a torrent of unwarranted abuse, "Who are you to ask me?" they exclaimed, their voice nearly a shout.

For both friends, this was an affront not only to their dignity but also to the very principles of equality of status enshrined in the nation's Constitution of a newly independent country, particularly from representatives of the the elected government, who are paid for the welfare of the people.

Determined to contest this injustice, they approached the train guard. The guard promptly summoned the inspector and enquired, "What is your justification for evacuating this coach?" Caught off guard, the inspector revealed, "A special shipment of *ten crore* (Hundred Million) rupees from the government treasury was in a separate coach attached to the train; we are on duty to safeguard it," he explained.

"While many passengers and Guards Were convinced by the revelation, Chinmay's deep understanding of constitutional evolution and the rule of law made him uneasy. "This information was meant to remain classified," he declared firmly. By disclosing it, you have breached the Government of India Official Secrets Act of 1923."

He explained further, "All of you intended to rest in a fully evacuated coach, while the lone guard at the rear—unrelated to this government treasury, even if he had no responsibility for it-would face all the risks." Now that everyone knows where the money is, criminals could easily overpower a solitary guard and detach the sealed coach, leaving all of you, the responsible officers, undisturbed and sleeping in the coach."

Addressing the guard, Chinmay added, "There is an urgent inquiry to determine if this violation was deliberate?"

Recognising the gravity of the breach, the guard asked the police officer to call the Superintendent of Police; otherwise, he would not allow the train to depart with a green signal.

The situation reversed within a few moments. Police officials apologised to the passengers and the guard, and no one was willing to compromise without reporting the matter to the Superintendent of Police.

Amid mounting pressure, Chinmay suggested a solution: the police officers would share the coach with civilian passengers. This measure would also ensure that at least one-third of the officers remained alert at all times, with two policemen rotating duty in the guard's cabin on each coach gate. The police team had no other option but to accept the proposal immediately.

This ingenious resolution earned Chinmay quiet acclaim among the passengers and even from the police officials themselves, who, in a rare moment of humility, saluted his integrity and astute understanding of government affairs and procedures at this early stage.

It was the second practical demonstration for Ramveer on how to manage a situation practically with knowledge and presence of mind.

After returning from vacation, they both decided to pursue the post-graduation program. During this time, the Union Public Service Commission announced exam results. Surprisingly, both were selected for one of the toughest exams. Only four more candidates from their campus advanced to this prestigious university's final round that year.

The news spread across the university campus. Amidst hundreds of congratulatory messages, several allies emerged. With the support of professors and senior students, both began preparing for their interviews.

Conversations had become longer, more rational, and pragmatic. The caste-based prejudice that had once plagued Ramveer had undergone a remarkable transformation. Those who once avoided speaking to him now visited his room for discussions and debates.

Amidst all these changes, the two collaborators remained steadfastly focused on their goals, immersed in fundamental questions and deep contemplation, undaunted by expectations or vested interests.

In the interview, Chinmay excelled with remarkable poise, while Ramveer's performance was average. Chinmay's self-assurance grew after the interview, particularly regarding his colleague, as he believed that his benevolent intervention, ensuring Ramveer's admit card was categorised in a way that would benefit him, had secured his friend's success.

After the civil service interview, both friends opted for different postgraduate streams. Chinmay is interested in resource distribution and enrolled in economics. Ramveer, guided by a quieter intensity, chose the path of law. For him, the Constitution was not just a document but a doorway to dignity.

A few weeks after starting their studies, a letter in Shivraman's handwriting came unexpectedly. Ramveer's father, Budhai, was gravely ill. Ramveer left university, returning to his village for two weeks. By the time he arrived, doctors had already started treatment, and under their steady hands, Budhai began to recover—his breathing eased. The cloud of uncertainty that hung over their modest home slowly began to lift.

Meanwhile, the much-awaited final results of the civil service examination were released. In the bustling corridors of Allahabad University, Chinmay rushed to check the list, his heart pounding with a mix of hope and certainty. But what he saw struck him with a silent weight. His name was absent.

This unforeseen outcome shattered Chinmay. The shock plunged him into a psychological maelstrom; an ocean of unbearable fury and searing pain gradually engulfed him. Once resolute and vibrant, his very being began to dissolve under the relentless tide of anguish. Each wave of torment battered his heart, eroding any vestige of hope until only despair remained—a poignant testament to the profound depths of human suffering.

Tormented by guilt over a secret intervention intended to help, he found himself unable to face Ramveer. In despair, he abruptly left Allahabad for his maternal uncle's home.

At the hostel, a postman arrived with Ramveer's joining letter, igniting the community's excitement about his accomplishment. Ramveer cleared the examination and secured the top position in the reserved category.

After reaching the campus, Ramveer scrutinised the list of successful candidates, and a haunting void gripped him—Chinmay's name was conspicuously absent. Moreover, he was shocked to learn that Chinmay was not on the campus either. Despite his repeated efforts to find a trace of his dear friend, there was no sign of Chinmay at the hostel or the university campus.

This triumph was a bittersweet and painful experience for Ramveer. Instead of rejoicing in his unprecedented success, he was tormented by the thought that his existence now seemed meaningless if fate had chosen him in this manner. Disregarding the congratulatory messages and media attention, his sole resolve was to return to his village to search for Chinmay.

The next day, he returned to the village to find out about Chinmay's whereabouts, but no one knew about Chinmay. While his community celebrated his achievement with resounding fervour, Ramveer was lost in the depths of his desolation within a modest hut, thinking about tearing apart the joining letter due to an unprecedented struggle and hard work.

Disturbed by Chinmay's sudden disappearance, Shivraman summoned Ramveer to reveal his whereabouts. But upon seeing Ramveer's condition, he sensed that the young man was overwhelmed by deep anguish and unable to speak.

Shivraman comforted him softly, "You need to go to Allahabad immediately. If you find out anything about Chinmay, let me know instantly. Meanwhile, I will work out through our relatives."

A few days after Ramveer arrived in Allahabad, he received a letter from Shivraman. The letter revealed that Chinmay was unwell and staying at his maternal uncle's home. According to the letter, Chinmay assured Ramveer that he would return to campus as soon as he recovered. The letter also reminded Ramveer that he must ensure he joins his Civil Services training on time.

Though hesitant and weighed down by grief, Ramveer, with a heavy heart yet firm resolve, decided to partake in his training. He was committed to honouring his journey and the unarticulated mission of reconnecting with Chinmay.

CHAPTER VII

Shadows of Doubt: The Science & Society

Perched high in the mist-shrouded hills of Mussoorie, the National Academy of Administration stood as both sanctuary and crucible, shaping the stewards of a newly sovereign India. The Academy was located in beautiful old buildings covered in ivy, with well-kept lawns. It had a special charm that showed both its history and its growth.

Each morning began before sunrise, as the sharp clang of a brass bell stirred the air. Clad in regulation tracksuits, probationers assembled for physical training on dew-soaked fields, their breath misting in the cold Himalayan air. The scent of pine mingled with the quiet resolve of young men and women drawn from every corner of the country—some fresh from university, others hardened by struggle—united by a common dream of service.

In the lecture halls, sunlight filtered through tall windows as retired bureaucrats, academics, and public intellectuals delivered constitutional law, public administration, and development economics lessons. The pedagogy combined the remnants of colonial rigour with a new spirit of democratic inquiry—rote memorisation gradually gave way to lively debates on ethics, social dynamics, governance, and the state's role in a free society.

Afternoons brought field studies and group projects, while evenings softened the day's discipline. Friendships were forged around fireplaces or under starlit verandas over tea and spirited discussions—on Neta ji Subhas's vision, Gandhi's relevance, or the promise and perils of planned development. Here, the making of a civil servant was not merely an intellectual pursuit but a moral and emotional awakening.

Ramveer stood at the threshold of the dining hall, the aroma of spiced lentils and *basmati rice* wafting toward him. It was his first time navigating this unfamiliar world without Chinmay beside him—the mentor cum companion who had guided, protected, and channelled his energies to academic excellence. All those dreams they shared, all those wishes of pure hearts, are now a reality before Ramveer, but the price he paid is beyond his mortal ken—a sacrifice so profound that it echoes across the fabric of his existence. Ramveer responded to every greeting with a forced smile that rarely reached his eyes.

He gradually adapted to his new environment, but his restlessness only increased. It felt as though being born into Budhai and Tulsa's *Dalit* family had marked him with an invisible sin—one he yearned to overcome through achievement. It felt as if the stigma of being Dalit had vanished instantly, as if he had been sanctified in that moment; he had been selected for the All-India Services. However, the same greetings and expressions of respect felt like a burden in his mind. It was an honour bestowed upon him due to his position rather than his talent. If it had recognised merit, Chinmay would have been by his side, even if it had taken him a little longer to reach this dreamland.

Ramveer's inner world was a mosaic of contradictions. Born into a Dalit community yet rising through sheer merit, he straddled divergent realms. In the refined corridors of upper-caste circles, he discussed society's broader perspectives, nationalism, global order, and class struggle. Despite the occasional humiliations that Chinmay typically helped him deflect, he felt intellectually stimulated in this environment. Conversely, within the informal gatherings of the Dalit community, conversations were often steeped in class struggle and occasionally veered into overt hostility, leaving him feeling alienated as these discussions strayed far from his vision of an inclusive social order. Caught between these conflicting worlds, he stood alone, burdened with the choice of where he truly belonged. Though he was fully aware that, given the prevailing social conditions, it was inevitable for the flames of rebellion to ignite among the Dalits due to the persistent injustices they faced, he did not place the blame solely on a single class. Instead, he perceived society's ignorant belief system as responsible for this state of affairs. He had often faced humiliation at the hands of his community, which belittled him. Even his father did not support his education, driven by deep-seated beliefs. In contrast, he had witnessed several members of the so-called upper castes striving earnestly for the upliftment of Dalits.

Moreover, Ramveer began to perceive a new caste system emerging within the hallowed institutions of excellence that masqueraded as a meritocracy. Even in this modern hierarchy, the pinnacle remained with the Indian Administrative Service, an elite class whose status was cemented by constitutional legitimacy. Regardless of one's talent, a narrow miss on the examination meant permanent exclusion from this revered lineage.

For the first time, he could visualise a continuum of class transformation: the ancient varna, initially based on functional roles, had gradually hardened into a rigid, birth-based hierarchy, only to be reinvented now under the guise of merit. Despite the societal neglect and exclusion he had endured as a *Dalit*, Ramveer harboured no resentment toward the upper castes. Instead, he grew increasingly uneasy with the overtly hostile interactions within both realms.

During his training, in the absence of Chinmay, a constant bridge to the upper-class milieu, Ramveer was isolated and unwelcome in those circles. With few alternatives and a deep yearning for genuine acceptance, he ultimately began associating more closely with the informal circle of his community. This reluctant choice underscored the paradox of his existence as he struggled to reconcile his ambitions with the complex realities of class, identity, and belonging.

During the Foundation Course, the visiting faculty led an interactive session on the origins of the Indian caste system and avenues for social inclusion. This academic foray set the stage for a day of reflective dialogue among officer trainees, aimed at shaping their approach to inclusive decision-making from a constitutional perspective.

Later that evening, informal conversations resumed over tea; a group of trainees gathered to continue the discussion from the morning, all coming from similar *Dalit* (untouchables) backgrounds. Among them was Chandran, a scholar from Tamil Nadu known for his unwavering scientific rigour. With a measured yet striking voice, he observed, "The caste system has been orchestrated so meticulously that it leaves no room for *Dalits* to emerge."

Chandran's eyes shone with conviction as he continued, "But change is not beyond our reach. History is filled with untold transformations, hidden in the folds of unwritten narratives. Consider the power of genetic diversity: if you reflect on Darwin's theory of evolution or Mendel's principles of inheritance, you'll notice that cross-cultural unions often produce offspring with greater genetic strength and intellectual ability. This shows that forging alliances with higher castes could enrich our generations and challenge the hierarchies that confine us."

The room fell silent as his audacious proposal enveloped the group like a dense fog. Eventually, Ramveer broke the silence, questioning sharply, "But who would permit such unions? We are untouchable beyond the boundaries of these few rare institutions of excellence."

Chandran's reply was incisive and unyielding. "When formal channels close, alternative paths must be pursued. History demonstrates that children from diverse unions, such as those born to monarchs from informal relationships across different castes, often exhibit exceptional traits, and society ultimately acknowledges them as relatively higher in caste; at the very least, they are not considered untouchables."

Chandran's words struck the assembly like a stone cast into still water. Discomfort rippled through the group; many recoiled, condemning the suggestion as socially unacceptable and fundamentally immoral. The discussion abruptly dissolved, leaving behind an air of unresolved tension and the lingering question of whether change, however audacious, was indeed within reach.

Later that night, Ramveer lay awake, reflecting on Chandran's words. Mendel and Darwin were remarkable scientists who significantly contributed to plant and animal reproduction. However, are their findings relevant to the social sciences, especially regarding humans? Studying human behaviour is exceedingly difficult, requiring immense data to create a reliable model - something even today's scientists find nearly impossible. His thoughts shifted to his family: his parents and siblings shared similar physical traits, including body structure and colour. Yet, none exhibited the same drive or curiosity he possessed. He attempted to articulate and compare his traits —stature, colour, and various other characteristics —with those of his family members, which made his quest for understanding increasingly complex.

Later, he reflected on Chinmay's family and recognised the traits the siblings and their parents shared. He had many similarities with Chinmay in thought processes, complexion, and body stature. In the chilly atmosphere, Ramveer, oblivious to the influence of his surroundings, started to tremble and sweat heavily very late in the night.

He woke up very late, thank God. It was a Sunday. Yet, he couldn't decide about the sudden burst of doubt that had come in the night. Many incidents suddenly disturbed him about Dadda (Shivraman), who had been his role model until then. Over the next few days, Ramveer couldn't shake the feeling. He began to notice things—how Dadda looked at him sometimes, with a mix of pride and something else.

For weeks afterwards, he lingered in the library in the late evening, trying to understand Darwin's theory of evolution and Mendel's principles of inheritance, comparing his traits with those of his parents and Shivraman. In this quest, a devastating pattern emerged—his personality, intellectual tendencies, and even some of his mannerisms mirrored those of Chinmay far more closely than those of anyone in his family. The implications filled him with a mixture of revelation and revulsion. His respect for Chinmay and his father, Shivraman, once boundless, crumbled under the weight of this terrible suspicion.

Cultural & Contextual Glossary:

Assistant Collector: An administrative post in India responsible for local revenue collection and governance, often regarded as a key early-career position in the civil services.

Foundation Course: In this context, an academic program for officer trainees that explores the origins of the Indian caste system and examines pathways toward social inclusion.

Dharma: A multifaceted concept in Indian philosophy, referring to duty, righteousness, and the moral order governing individual conduct and the cosmic balance.

Varna System: This ancient framework divided society into four primary groups—Brahmins, Kshatriyas, Vaishyas, and Shudras—and laid the foundation for the modern caste system in India.

Basmati Rice: A variety of long-grain rice from India with an aromatic distinction from other rice varieties and tastes.

CHAPTER VIII

Emerging from the Ashes: Redefining Destiny

Chinmay has descended to the lowest depths of emotional and psychological turmoil for months, even losing awareness of his daily routine, which has created concern for his family. Understanding the seriousness of his condition, doctors referred him to a hospital in Delhi for treatment.

After some time, he began to recover physically, and he embarked on a period of deep introspection. Amidst the lingering echoes of a painful past—the heavy weight of tradition and the constant struggle for recognition—a small, persistent light began to break through the darkness, guiding him toward a path of progressive betterment, when one incredible evening, as his family gathered around a dinner table adorned with gleaming brass plates—a relic of tradition—a distinguished guest arrived.

It was his mother's cousin, an officer in the Ministry of Education, whose presence exuded both warmth and authority. His presence carried the warmth of familial affection and the quiet understanding of a man who had seen the world beyond the narrow lanes of mindset in which Chinmay was suffering.

With a courteous nod and a hint of a smile, the guest began sharing his experiences abroad and options for higher studies. During the discussion, he learned about Chinmay, including his academic achievements and success in the ICS mains exam on his first attempt and the educational rankings of the pathways leading to his graduation. Impressed by Chinmay's accomplishments, he spoke about the Rhodes Scholarship—a prestigious program that has opened doors for Indian students to pursue advanced studies abroad. His words lingered in the air, resonating with promise and possibility. These insights became a turning point in Chinmay's life, opening his eyes to a world beyond his vision and inspiring him to dream big.

"You have the mind for it, Chinmay," the maternal uncle declared gently and insistently. "Your circumstances here should never confine your destiny. The Rhodes Scholarship could transform your life, enabling you to study at Oxford and bring back the wisdom that will guide us all and perhaps a significant portion of our society. This revelation, laden with promise and possibility, kindled a flicker of hope in Chinmay's heart, inviting him to envision a future where his academic journey might transcend the familiar confines of home.

That night, for the first time in a long time, Chinmay felt a spark of hope stir within him—a fragile yet unyielding spark of ambition. In the quiet solitude that followed the family's parting, he retraced every conversation and every unspoken longing accumulated over the years of struggle. The idea of transcending the familiar borders of his village, of stepping into a world of academic excellence and global dialogue, filled him with both trepidation and exhilaration.

In the following days, Chinmay found himself drawn into an unexpected whirlwind. He began to meticulously gather documents, personal statements, and academic records, preparing a formidable application for the Rhodes Scholarship. His mind, once preoccupied with the mundane details of everyday survival, now soared with visions of Oxford's Gothic spires, classrooms steeped in centuries of scholarship, and the vibrant mosaic of cultures interwoven within its ancient halls.

Chinmay tried to keep his interactions on the university campus to a bare minimum, but news of his unusual decision spread throughout the campus. Professors, classmates, and even erstwhile friends could not help but express their opinions. Some cautioned him gently, reminding him of the secure path before him—a promising career in the civil services, a future already sketched out in letters and traditions. Others, more overt in their scepticism, whispered that his aspirations were but flights of fancy. Yet, even as these voices rose around him, Chinmay listened quietly, his resolve deepening with every murmur of dissent.

He recalled vividly how his heart had always harboured a silent sense of superiority—a quiet conviction that his intellect, honed by years of clandestine study and the earnest tutoring he had offered to his friend Ramveer, could not be measured by the narrow metrics of conventional success. Working in the civil service, particularly in a junior role, would humiliate his inner dignity. His aspirations were not mere echoes of inherited privilege; they were the product of sleepless nights, fervent dreams, and the burning desire to break free from a social order that had long defined him by his circumstances.

Thus, Chinmay plunged into the arduous preparation process for an entirely different future. He balanced his academic commitments with rigorous preparation for the Oxford entrance exams, dedicating countless hours to study and reflection. Over six challenging months, he mastered the intricacies of the GMAT, painstakingly compiled his academic transcripts, and crafted personal statements that revealed not only his intellect but also the scars of his past—a testament to a life lived at the intersection of ambition and adversity. Letters of recommendation from esteemed professors lent weight to his application, each one a subtle affirmation of the promise he embodied.

The process, daunting as it was, soon became a source of solace. Each challenge met and each document perfected served to displace the lingering shadows of past traumas with the bright light of possibility. It was as if every obstacle was a stepping stone, gradually constructing a pathway to a future that defied the limitations imposed by birth and tradition.

Then, one crisp morning, the moment of destiny arrived. An official envelope, bearing international postage and the unmistakable seal of academic authority, arrived at his modest doorstep. With trembling hands and a racing heart, Chinmay opened the letter. The words on the page confirmed what he had dared to hope—he had been awarded the Rhodes Scholarship for an economics program at the University of Oxford. Overwhelmed with joy and disbelief, Chinmay could hardly contain his emotions.

In that instant, the entire village seemed to come alive with jubilation. Children, who had never strayed far from their homes, gaped in wonder at the thought of a land as distant and mystical as England. Elders, whose lives had been shaped by India's tumultuous struggle for independence, watched with pride and a touch of disbelief as one of their own prepared to cross oceans in pursuit of knowledge.

Upon arriving at the historic grounds of Oxford, he experienced a profound mixture of alienation and belonging. The ancient Gothic architecture, the profound silence of revered halls, and the diverse mosaic of international students stood in stark contrast to the dusty streets of his Uttar Pradesh village. Yet, he found a haven for his intellect within this esteemed institution. In this environment, every lecture and debate echoed the potential for change, instilling in him a sense of anticipation and excitement for what lay ahead.

At Oxford, a new Chapter began in Chinmay's life, marked by relentless pursuit, intellectual bravery, and the quiet yet powerful defiance of fate. In every lecture, conversation, and late-night study session, he carried the dreams for his own country, the weight of history, and an unyielding desire to redefine destiny. As he forged on this journey, he knew that his achievements were not solely for himself but for every soul who had ever dared to dream of a better tomorrow.

Under the mentorship of distinguished economists, Chinmay delved into the realms of development economics, monetary policy, and the intricacies of economic reform. His firsthand experiences of rural poverty and social exclusion lent a rare depth to theoretical discussions, bridging the gap between abstract ideas and the real challenges faced by communities in his home country. Professors marvelled at his ability to illuminate complex concepts with clarity and insight, remarking that his perspectives were as transformative as they were unexpected.

CHAPTER IX

Yearning for a Child

A few months later, after Ramveer had taken his post as Assistant Collector, his parents, Tulsa and Budhai, arranged his marriage to Kanchan, the beautiful daughter of a Member of Parliament from Bihar. The wedding was a grand affair as opposed to the community standard, though upper-caste guests from the village were conspicuously absent, except for one brief appearance.

Ramveer stood beside Kanchan at their wedding, the ceremony a blur of colours and sounds. His parents, Tulsa and Budhai, beamed with pride, their faces glowing under the marigold garlands. The hall was filled with guests, but the absence of upper-caste faces was palpable, except for one. Shivraman appeared briefly, his presence commanding despite his understated demeanour. He approached the couple, his expression unreadable. 'May your union be blessed with joy and purpose,' he said, placing a hand on Ramveer's head. The touch was brief, but it sent a shock through Ramveer. He looked up, and for a moment, their eyes met. In that instant, he saw regret, perhaps, or recognition. Did Shivraman know what he was thinking?

As Shivraman turned to leave, Ramveer felt a pang of loss, of betrayal, though he couldn't say why. The man who had been his role model was now a question mark in his life, a puzzle he didn't want to rethink.

The government bungalow that welcomed Ramveer's parents and his wife provided them with comforts unimaginable compared to their village life. Initially restless in this new leisure world, his father soon found purpose among the soil and seedlings. Within weeks, his weathered hands had transformed the useless area, with countless thorny plants, into a magnificent garden of flowers that drew admiring glances from passersby. The backyard, once barren, now flourished with vegetables that reminded them all of their rural roots.

Yet, his mother's stunning transformation had stirred Ramveer to his core. In the flickering reels of his childhood memories, *Amma* had primarily been a mere shadow, rising before dawn to whip up meals, vanishing into the fields until dusk, her essence overshadowed by his older sisters, who filled in the void of her absence. How often had he stood in awe as she toiled at *Dadda's* (Shivraman) home, serving Janki Devi, cleaning, and nurturing cows with her head bowed and hands worn from labour?

Now, as she moved through his bungalow with unexpected grace, Ramveer often blinked in disbelief. Was this elegant woman with fair skin, no longer darkened by relentless sun, indeed the same mother he had known? She arranged flowers in crystal vases, received guests with quiet confidence, and prepared dishes that rivalled those served in the homes of his colleagues. Sometimes, observing her from his study doorway, he could have sworn he was watching Janki Devi, as if she were herself, as though her master's mother had not merely learned skills but absorbed the essence of the educated woman she had served.

"Modern educated females could learn much from your mother," a few guests commented, usually on her common sense and hospitality. She had almost all the recipes and processes for the intricate art of preparing festive sweets that had once been the speciality of Chinmay's household.

On a leisurely Sunday afternoon, as Ramveer worked on important office correspondence, he overheard a discussion that would profoundly reshape his views on inheritance, extending beyond his scientific training and knowledge of Mendel and Darwin's theories.

"The secret is in the yearning," his mother whispered to Kanchan, who sat with protectively folded hands over her still-flat abdomen. "When you yearn for a child, you must hold a vision clear as mountain water. See the face, the mind, the heart you wish to create."

Kanchan leaned closer, hungry for this wisdom that no doctor had offered.

"*Malkin* taught me this when I served in her home," Tulsa continued, her voice soft with reverence as she recalled the lessons from her time working with Janki Devi. She told me that if I wished for a son for a long time and yearned for a childlike Lord Krishna—clever, compassionate, and beautiful—such qualities would manifest in the child. While working in their home, sweeping the floors, I would close my eyes and picture a boy with Chinmay's brilliance—how that child's mind seemed to grasp everything it encountered! Within a year, the gods blessed us with Ramveer.

She smiled, smoothing Kanchan's sari. "You have not seen Chinmay. The same intelligence shines in their eyes, the same quickness of thought. Chinmay went to America, a land of untold riches across the ocean. Perhaps this government position is not grand enough for that brilliant boy." Tulsa continued after a pause, "I'm not sure whether Ramveer shared this with you, but it was Chinmay's resolution and undeniable support that forced the school management to admit Ramveer."

Ramveer's pen hovered motionless above his papers. The scientific principles that had structured his education—Darwin's theory of natural selection and Mendel's theory of genetic inheritance—suddenly seemed like hollow frameworks that failed to capture the human's profound power of imagination; in fact, this yearning differentiates humans from others. What laboratory could measure a mother's yearning? What equation could calculate the shaping force of a woman who, though unable to read a single word, had been imagining and urging for a brilliance into being while her hands worked the soil and scrubbed the floors?

This episode humbled him. His academic achievements, his government position, and his rational understanding of the world all paled in comparison to the wisdom of yearning, a silent determination of women who dreamed of better worlds. It was the first time Ramveer had understood the power of human consciousness and the ability to create favourable conditions even after dormancy for many years.

At the same time, he also feels guilty, as he has been misunderstood in some social relationships and misinterpreted in the light of a scientific phenomenon propagated by Chandran. With half-baked knowledge, he silently accused his loved ones within his heart. Today, respect for Shivraman and his family was at its zenith in his heart and mind. He felt an impulsive urge to talk to his mentor, guardian, and friend Chinmay again, with whom he had had no contact for almost one and a half years. He knew he still loved him more than his own life, but suddenly, a pang of guilt crept into his mind, and it seemed he was responsible for everything, even Chinmay's failure in the civil services examination.

He watched silently that night as Kanchan slept beside him. Ramveer wondered what visions she might be crafting in her dreams and what child she might already be forming in the crucible of her yearning—a continuation not just of bloodlines but of aspirations that transcended and decided the passing of genes.

CULTURAL & CONTEXTUAL GLOSSARY:

Malkin: an address by workers used for their female upper-caste employer.
Amaa: word used for mother in India

CHAPTER X

A Transformation: From Local to Global

Chinmay completed his MSc with Honours from the University of Oxford. Following his strong academic performance, he pursued a Master of Philosophy (MPhil) in Economics. His thesis on agricultural reform policies for developing economies received special commendation and was later published in reputable academic journals. Subsequently, Chinmay was recruited by the International Monetary Fund (IMF) through its prestigious Economist Program, which seeks to attract exceptional talent worldwide.

He became one of the youngest economists to join the organisation and one of the few from a developing nation.

The IMF headquarters in Washington, D.C., presented yet another cultural adjustment. The imposing building on 19th Street housed some of the world's most influential economic minds. Chinmay's initial assignment placed him in the Asia and Pacific Department, where he worked on assessments of regional economies.

His early work focused on balance of payments issues in Southeast Asian economies. Colleagues admired his meticulous attention to detail and ability to integrate economic data with broader social and political analyses, setting him apart in an institution often focused on purely technical assessments.

By this time, Chinmay had been promoted to a senior economist position, and his expertise in agricultural economics and rural development provided him with a unique perspective on how oil price shocks impacted food security and rural economies in developing nations.

During a critical staff meeting, Chinmay challenged the conventional IMF approach to the crisis. While many of his colleagues focused on standard stabilisation packages, emphasising fiscal restraint, Chinmay argued for more nuanced approaches for agricultural economies.

He reportedly stated during the meetings, "If we impose severe austerity on economies where most people live on subsistence farming, we risk creating humanitarian crises that will ultimately undermine economic stability. " His intervention led to the formation of a specialised working group on food security within the IMF's policy framework.

The IMF's Managing Director at the time noticed the young Indian economist's insights. In his memoirs, he wrote: "Among our diverse staff, there were a few who understood that economic formulas must adapt to human realities. Chinmay was foremost among them—he could speak the language of sophisticated economic modelling while never forgetting the farmers and workers whose lives our policies affected."

Chinmay's most significant contribution during this period came with his involvement in designing the Extended Fund Facility (EFF). This innovative financing mechanism was designed to provide medium-term support to countries facing significant payment imbalances resulting from structural impediments or slow economic growth.

Drawing on his experiences in rural India, Chinmay advocated for extended repayment periods and gradual adjustment paths for developing economies. He argued that structural transformations required time and that too-rapid adjustment could create social instability, ultimately undermining economic reforms.

"The EFF represented a philosophical shift in how we approached economic assistance," Chinmay explained in various lectures and columns at the delivered various institutions. We recognised that some economic challenges were structural, not cyclical, and required patience and ongoing support.

The facility became a cornerstone of IMF lending operations, and many of Chinmay's innovations in program design continued to influence IMF approaches decades later. His work during this period earned him the IMF Excellence in Economic Research Award, the first time the honour had been bestowed upon an economist from a developing nation.

Later, for almost a decade, Chinmay participated in numerous IMF missions to countries across Asia, Africa, and Latin America. These field experiences profoundly shaped his economic thinking and reinforced his commitment to practical, context-sensitive solutions.

A mission to drought-stricken countries in the Sahel region of Africa proved particularly formative. Witnessing climate vulnerability, economic fragility, and institutional challenges, Chinmay developed a framework for assessing economic resilience that incorporated environmental sustainability decades before it became mainstream in economic thinking.

During a mission to Thailand, Chinmay spent weeks travelling through rural provinces, meeting with farmers, local officials, and agricultural cooperatives. His mission report included detailed analyses of how national-level economic policies translated to village-level impacts—an unusual approach for IMF documents of that era.

Dr. Elizabeth Montgomery, who worked with him on several missions, expressed her view on Chinmay during a discussion with a few senior journalists: "Most economists saw only numbers on spreadsheets. Chinmay saw the human stories behind those numbers. He would include details about local agricultural practices, informal credit systems, and community support networks that most of us overlooked."

This approach sometimes created tension with colleagues who preferred more traditional macroeconomic analyses. Still, it earned him respect among officials in developing countries who felt that Chinmay truly understood their challenges.

The Debt Crisis and Structural Adjustment Era brought new challenges as the developing world plunged into a debt crisis. Many countries that had borrowed heavily found themselves unable to meet their obligations as interest rates rose and commodity prices fell. The IMF and World Bank responded with structural adjustment programs, which became controversial due to their social impacts.

By then, Chinmay had been promoted to Division Chief in the Policy Development and Review Department, where he had significant influence over program design and development. His position placed him at the centre of debates about how the IMF should respond to the debt crisis.

While he supported the need for fiscal discipline and market-oriented reforms, he consistently advocated for more gradual implementation timelines, stronger social safety nets, and protection for essential public services.

In a confidential memo to management, he wrote, "Our adjustment programs must recognise the political and social realities of implementing difficult reforms. If we push too hard and fast, we risk creating conditions that make reform politically untenable. A failed reform is worse than a gradual reform."

This perspective led him to develop what became known internally as the "Chinmay Sequencing Framework"—a methodical structural and functional approach to implementing reforms prioritising building institutional capacity and social protection before undertaking the most disruptive market liberalisation measures.

CHAPTER XI

Time of Reconnection: Value of Silence

Ramveer has had the fantastic opportunity to serve as a collector in many districts, always striving to maximise his potential. Unlike many of his colleagues, he finds little interest in wealth creation; what he has earned far exceeds his dreams from his early life. His home life is filled with harmony and satisfaction, thanks to the perfect balance provided by Dadda (Father), Amma (Mother), and his beloved wife Kanchan. Together, they've created a warm, peaceful haven, beautifully arranged with high-quality, handmade treasures. All the helpers in their home are treated respectfully, often receiving fresh vegetables from their backyard garden. Occasionally, Kanchan takes the time to teach their kids, sharing her knowledge and love for learning during her free moments.

Each posting provided valuable insights for Ramveer's professional development. He recognised how effective water management systems could significantly impact the well-being of communities in drought-affected Bundelkhand. In the industrial regions of western Uttar Pradesh, he observed the direct correlation between well-formulated policies and economic progress. His experiences in the remote hilly districts enabled him to appreciate the critical balance between safeguarding cultural heritage and fostering development. Through these experiences, Ramveer gained a nuanced understanding of the subcontinent's social, cultural, and geographical complexities. He realised that effective policymaking must extend beyond central directives; it requires an alignment with the unique natural and cultural contexts of the communities it aims to serve. To achieve this, the Planning Commission must develop district-specific development models, integrating them into a cohesive, coordinated strategy.

His wife, Kanchan, often teased him about his transformation. "You were going to be a rebel poet once," she would say, smiling as she adjusted his tie before important meetings. "Now look at you—the government's perfect problem-solver."

"Perfect is a dangerous word," Ramveer would always reply, but he couldn't deny the satisfaction his work brought him. Each solution was implemented, each system improved, and each life made better.

After distinguished service as a district collector in various regions and other field positions, Ramveer was elevated to Additional Secretary in the Ministry of Finance. In this role, he coordinated with the Planning Commission, the Ministry of Finance, and various other organisations to shape policy frameworks for development projects and resource management.

This was a tough time wherein country was crippling economic crisis with currency reserves at an all-time low. Rumours of decline swirled through the streets, whispered in crowded bazaars and echoed within the hallowed halls of government. This crisis was not a sudden anomaly but the culmination of decades of neglect and the gradual erosion of time-tested institutions. In an atmosphere of scarce hope, the nation yearned for a visionary to steer it back to prosperity.

Amid mounting political instability, the new Prime Minister convened an emergency meeting of civil service officials, urging everyone to brainstorm solutions to pull the economy from the brink. After a long, deliberate debate and discussion among senior officials and ministers on the economic conditions, they concluded on an emergency bailout package from the IMF. Being a relatively junior official, Ramveer listened carefully to everyone, finally decided to speak, and asked for permission at the end of the meeting.

Getting the permission, he started with a balanced, modest voice filled with unusual passion. "Our problem isn't merely economic or financial—it's structural and functional. We've built an economic system that rewards complacency and penalises innovation without regard for long-term development. We need not just a bailout or a loan; we must reconfigure our entire economic architecture and structural and functional reforms at this critical juncture." Even the finance minister—a seasoned economist—nodded thoughtfully in agreement.

Having carefully studied Ramveer's insights, the Prime Minister remarked, "You've identified the disease rather than just the symptoms. I want you to lead this effort." Recognising the gravity of his insight, the Prime Minister entrusted him with developing a comprehensive strategy for overhauling the administrative machinery and the broader policy framework.

Humbly, Ramveer responded, "Being a civil servant, I have extensive expertise in policy implementation, and I can identify gaps in our current framework and suggest improvements." However, structural and functional changes in our policy and governance require an experienced professional exposed to proven models of modern economic development." The Prime Minister replied, "Then find someone trustworthy who can start as soon as possible." He added that the Minister of Finance would have the final authority to make this appointment and to assemble the necessary team.

Later that evening, the finance minister called Ramveer for suggestions on an expert in developmental economics to serve on the Committee on Economic Affairs. As they discussed, a name surfaced from the depths of Ramveer's memory. "Chinmay," he whispered. "He's the only Indian with extensive experience on various global projects in developing economies at the IMF."

The very next day, the Ministry of Finance extended an offer to Chinmay to join as an economic advisor, marking the beginning of a new chapter in the nation's quest for structural reform and sustainable growth.

Over the following days, Ramveer buried himself in work, yet memoirs of a long-lost bond persisted. He recalled debates and discussions with Chinmay about their vision for society in the bustling university canteen, late-night study sessions in their cramped hostel, and the fervent plans they once made to transform India together. A slight misunderstanding and mutual guilt had erected a silent wall between them, causing more than two decades of unintentional separation, despite no catastrophic fallout or unforgivable betrayal.

An acceptance letter from Chinmay succinctly stated, "I eagerly anticipate contributing to the nation's economic recovery; it would be a privilege for me."

In this time of deep perplexity, Ramveer resolved to break the silence. Determined to revive the bond that had once been their strength, he planned a grand, celebratory welcome for his old friend. He reached out to friends from graduation, reconnected with professors at Allahabad, and gathered the support of his family, Chinmay's parents, and siblings. As he feared that a private reunion after two decades might never fully erase the awkwardness of guilt, he believed that a public gathering—with witnesses and shared memories—could help them both emerge from isolation.

Unaware of this celebration, Chinmay reached Delhi by evening. Following all the proper protocols, a car arrived at his hotel to pick him up, leading him to believe that this dinner was an official one organised by ministry officials.

As soon as he entered the hall, he stood frozen in shock. He had never imagined seeing all his old friends and his parents; the memories he had left behind so long ago gathered in one place.

For a moment that seemed to stretch into eternity, Chinmay and Ramveer looked at each other across the crowded room. Chinmay, once lanky and carefree, now carried himself with the gravitas of someone who had counselled nations. His hair was silver at the temples, his face lined with experience, but his eyes-those same questioning, brilliant eyes—widened in recognition.

Ramveer made the first move, crossing the room with deliberate steps. The buzz of conversation dimmed as guests recognised the significance of the moment.

"Welcome home," Ramveer said, extending his hand.

Chinmay took the offered hand, catching sight of Ramveer's impassioned visage, and whispered as if unveiling a cherished secret, "Is this just a home? It's paradise for which I have yearned for over two decades." At these words, their souls drew together, and together, they surrendered to a torrent of tears—a silent cascade that spoke of promises fulfilled and dreams long awaited. It was a time to let go of old grievances, but what a surprise—it took only a few seconds to bridge the gap that had weighed so heavily on the hearts for years. This illustrates that when we possess unwavering faith and trust within our hearts, verbal communication becomes unnecessary for mutual understanding or being comprehended.

The embrace that followed was initially awkward and then fierce. Someone began to applaud, and soon, the entire room joined in. The parents, now in their eighties, share memories with wet eyes. Kanchan squeezed *Amma's* hand, and both women smiled through tears.

Later, as the evening progressed and the initial shock of reunion gave way to more relaxed conversations, Chinmay and Ramveer found themselves alone in a quiet corner of the hall.

"All these years, I should have reached out," Chinmay said.

"So should I," Ramveer admitted. But I convinced myself that you wouldn't want to hear from me.

"Why wouldn't I?" Chinmay asked, genuinely puzzled.

Ramveer looked down at his glass. "I think this was just guilt, but you went on to become exactly what we talked about—an economist who could change systems. I became part of the system instead."

Chinmay's laugh was unexpected. "Is that what you think? Ramveer, I've spent my career helping governments formulate and review their policy outcomes, while you've spent yours implementing them. We took different paths to the same destination."

"I never thought of it that way," Ramveer admitted.

Chinmay noted with excessive laughter, "This has always been our problem: we overanalyse rather than engage in a simple conversation."

Vikram, who had since become a university professor, had travelled from Allahabad to witness this long-awaited reunion of friends. Even today, he carried the weight of shame for the words that had once slipped out of his mouth during a spontaneous and informal debate in a hostel room. After much contemplation, he had come to see this gathering as the perfect moment to unburden himself from the guilt that had haunted him for years. Vikram stood before his friends with wet eyes and spoke, "Years ago, when I was an immature youth, I uttered..."

But before he could complete his sentence, sensing the moment's gravity, both friends interrupted, saying, "Perhaps it is because of the very incident that we are witnessing this remarkable occasion today. We are both deeply grateful to you. "Sometimes, words may taste bitter in the present, yet their repercussions can be truly extraordinary."

Now, with the wisdom of years, they could see its absurdity. Their friendship had never been a limitation—it had been a foundation. Both had achieved success in their absence but carried an emptiness that no accomplishment could fill.

The conversation among old friends seemed endless, filled with laughter and nostalgia. Stories flowed like wine—adventures forgotten, triumphs shared too late, sorrows weathered alone that should have been shouldered together.

As midnight approached, Chinmay raised his glass with a warm smile. "Here's to building a lasting family," he proposed. "May we always find our way back to each other."

Ultimately, they decided that a team led by Vikram would establish an alumni network at Allahabad University and devise a strategy to foster a living relationship with the university and professionals. This would enable all alumni to unite on a single platform within the next two years, driving social transformation by bridging gaps in various facets of development.

However, the actual resonance was set to begin the very next morning, when Ramveer and Chinmay would sit down at the Ministry of Finance to start work on realigning their nation's economic future. Their separate journeys had equipped them with complementary skills and perspectives. What they might have accomplished together in their youth was nothing compared to what they could now, seasoned by experience, tempered by challenges, and renewed by reconnection.

The night air was cool and clear as the guests departed and Ramveer walked Chinmay back to his car. Stars punctuated the darkness above, reminding both men of nights spent on the university rooftop, dreaming impossible dreams.

Chinmay murmured, 'In the endless flow of time, we have been given a rare gift—a chance to realise our long-held dreams.

Ramveer nodded. "Only a rare few receive such an opportunity."

"Then let's make the most of it," Chinmay responded, his voice gaining confidence. "Let's create something that will impact future generations."

As Chinmay's car disappeared into the night, Ramveer turned toward Kanchan, his parents, and the sanctuary that had sustained him through the years. Tomorrow would bring new challenges, new possibilities, and the revival of a collaboration that had been silent for decades.

CHAPTER XII

Gambit: A Battle Against Bureaucratic Rot

The fluorescent lights of the conference room hummed overhead as Chinmay massaged his temples, staring at the wall of data projected before him. It was 2:13 AM. They'd worked past midnight for the fourth consecutive night, but time had become an abstract concept in the race to save a nation from economic collapse. Scattered across the long table were stacks of reports from Maharashtra, Gujarat, Tamil Nadu—each state's fiscal anatomy dissected, analysed, and reconstructed on paper.

"Coffee?" Ramveer stood in the doorway, holding two steaming cups. His crumpled white shirt spoke of a long, demanding day, but it was the dark circles under his eyes that truly revealed his fatigue.

Chinmay accepted the cup gratefully. "Remember when we used to study like this for ICS exams? All night, surrounded by books, we were convinced that we were preparing for the greatest challenge of our careers.

Ramveer laughed, a warm, resonant sound that momentarily dispelled the weight of their task. "How innocent we were. "He gestured at the sprawling documentation of a faltering bureaucracy: "This is the actual exam."

"Punjab's report is finally done," Chinmay said, sliding a folder across the table. I've identified three significant projects where siphoning funds has been a custom for many decades, and the dates are being extended with foolish reasons being mentioned. The administrative costs alone are swallowing fifty per cent of the budget before it reaches the actual beneficiaries."

Ramveer nodded grimly, pulling up the file on his computer. "I've colour-coded the ministries based on their waste percentages. Red indicates departments where more than thirty per cent of allocation disappears into what I'm calling 'administrative black holes.'" He turned his computer screen toward Chinmay. Most of the chart glowed alarming crimson.

"The education ministry is particularly egregious," he continued. Schools that exist only on paper, teachers who never teach, and the absence of performance-based appraisal are not just inefficiency; they are industrial-scale corruption.

Chinmay leaned back in his chair, his eyes drifting to the window where the lights of New Delhi twinkled against the pre-dawn sky. Millions of citizens slept somewhere in that sprawling metropolis, unaware that two ageing youths were struggling to review and work for the very foundation of governance that teetered on the edge of failure.

A few weeks later, in early office hours, Ramveer said softly, "The Minister of Finance is expecting our presentation at sharp eleven O'clock in the Cabinet meeting chaired by the Prime Minister. He's one of the few who truly understands what we're trying to achieve."

"And other Ministers?" Chinmay asked with curiosity.

"Each one of them has their own opinions and justifications. But they'll come around when they see the IMF numbers." Ramveer replied with confidence.

The ministerial conference room buzzed with tension. Fourteen cabinet ministers sat in leather chairs around the oval table, some leaning forward with interest, while others crossed their arms defensively. At the head of the table, the Prime Minister observed silently, his expression unreadable.

Chinmay stood beside the presentation screen, his voice steady despite his fatigue. "The current system isn't merely inefficient—it's designed to fail. Our analysis reveals that sixty-three per cent of government processes primarily exist to sustain themselves rather than serve citizens.

A murmur rippled through the room. The fourth-generation politician, the agriculture minister whose family had built a dynasty on farmer subsidies, scoffed audibly, looking at the papers already shared with the ministers.

"What you propose is radical and untested," he declared. "Zero-based budgeting? Requiring every expenditure to be justified from scratch? It would paralyse operations."

"With respect, Minister," Chinmay interjected, his village accent still detectable beneath his polished diction, "what's paralysing operations is the current approach. Your ministry administers fourteen separate subsidy schemes, each with its own bureaucracy. Farmers must navigate eleven offices for basic assistance, while seventy per cent of allocated funds never reach them."

The minister's face flushed. "How dare you blame like this—"

"It's not a blame," Chinmay said, advancing to a slide showing an agricultural fund distribution flow chart. "It's a documented fact. And this pattern repeats across every ministry represented in this room."

The commerce minister leaned forward. Unlike many of his colleagues, he hails from South India and has experience working with intergovernmental organisations after completing his doctorate at MIT. He systematically understands administration and recognises systemic dysfunction when he sees it.

"What do you propose as an alternative?" he asked.

Chinmay smiled for the first time that morning. "Public-Private Partnership Models across Critical Sectors." We've identified potential partnerships for essential services that the government delivers inefficiently. He displayed a comprehensive diagram. In Infrastructure projects alone, we can increase service delivery by 34 per cent while reducing administrative costs by half.

Do you want to privatise government services? The Labour Minister's voice rose incredulously.

Chinmay handed over the presentation to Ramveer slowly, managing his posture to speak something very important. The room was heavy with the quiet rustle of papers and the faint ticking of the wall clock. Ministers and secretaries looked on, some curious, some cautious. Chinmay's voice, steady and deliberate, broke the silence.

"Honourable members, we must understand that the role of the government in this new age is no longer to produce goods or deliver every service on its own. That model has served its time. Today, our task is to build the right environment where industries, entrepreneurs, and service providers can thrive on the strength of their ideas and enterprise."

He paused, looking directly at a few senior ministers before continuing, "If we try to do everything ourselves, we will only limit competition and choke innovation. No matter how well-intentioned, state-led services often become slow, inefficient, and unable to meet the needs of a changing world.

Walking slowly to the edge of the table, Chinmay's tone deepened with conviction. "Let us step back from those areas where private players can deliver better, faster, and smarter. Let us give them the tools, not the chains—clear rules, strong infrastructure, and a level playing field. When we do that, we don't lose control—we gain progress."

He opened his file, glanced briefly, then looked up again. "Take China as an example. A decade ago, it began to free its private sector, offering them better infrastructure, simpler policies, and state support. Today, its factories power global markets. Its rise didn't come from controlling everything—it came from enabling growth."

Chinmay's final words were calm, but carried weight. "If we want our economy to rise—truly rise—we must trust our people, support our institutions, and create a system where excellence is not ordered from above but built from the ground up. Only then will India find her rightful place in the world."

He sat down quietly. The room was silent, not out of disagreement, but because the future he had laid out was difficult to ignore.

They presented their findings ministry by ministry, for hours, detailing waste, identifying redundancies, and proposing streamlined alternatives. Some ministers took furious notes; others sat in stony silence. The Prime Minister watched it all, occasionally asking incisive questions that suggested he understood the stakes better than most in the room.

As they concluded, the defence minister finally spoke. "This is academically interesting, but practically, such drastic changes seem impossible. Do you think the International Monetary Fund extends credit based on theoretical reforms? They want concrete outcomes."

Chinmay glanced at Ramveer and the Minister of Finance before retrieving a sealed envelope from his briefcase. "Minister, we've already had preliminary discussions with the IMF. Their assessment team reviewed our proposal last week, but given the grim economic situation, they require some collateral, that is, an assurance of commitment from the representatives of the country. This needs to be decided by the honourable members present at this meeting."

The room fell silent as he handed the document to the Prime Minister, who scanned it, his eyebrows rising slightly—the most emotion he had displayed throughout the meeting.

"The IMF has provisionally approved a stabilisation loan of $2.2 billion," the Prime Minister announced, "contingent upon implementing these reforms."

Once the IMF approved the loan, most ministers and government officials reverted to their usual ways of working, finding comfort in their routines. However, Ramveer and Chinmay focused on creating blueprints for more effective execution of key projects and processes, remaining dedicated to their mission. Despite facing ongoing resistance within various departments, they continued to provide essential support for implementing functional and structural reforms. They quietly challenged the status quo and worked to transform policy into tangible change, evident in Chinmay's office as he reviewed the latest implementation reports. Eight months into the reform program, resistance remained fierce, particularly among middle-level bureaucrats who mastered passive sabotage.

"A few states are still stonewalling the structural and functional reforms," Ramveer said, entering with a stack of files. The chief secretary there reassigned every official we trained in the new system.

Chinmay nodded wearily. "I expected as much. The local cartels have too much influence in many states. Even though we're making progress slowly."

Their workspace had evolved from a single conference room to an entire wing of the ministry building. Young analysts—many recruited directly from top universities—moved purposefully between workstations, analysing data, drafting policy revisions, and tracking implementation metrics. What had begun as a two-person crusade had become a movement, attracting idealistic reformers from within the bureaucracy who had long awaited such an opportunity.

"The railway PPP pilot in Maharashtra is showing remarkable results," Ramveer continued, his mood brightening. On-time performance increased by twenty-two per cent, maintenance costs decreased, and—most surprisingly—employee satisfaction improved once we eliminated the nested approval processes.

Chinmay allowed himself a small smile. "We need to document that thoroughly. Success stories are our most effective weapon against institutional inertia.

Their conversation was interrupted by a call from the Prime Minister's office. Major economic indicators have shown improvement for the second consecutive quarter. Growth was modest but genuine. Inflation had stabilised. Most importantly, tax compliance increased by nine per cent as simplified processes made evasion more difficult.

Later that evening, as they shared a rare moment of leisure on the balcony of Chinmay's apartment, watching the rain sweep across the city, Ramveer reflected on their journey.

"We've barely scratched the surface," he said. After two years of work, we've reformed perhaps just a few per cent of what needs changing. More interestingly, those political executives who initially opposed this reform have started taking credit for it openly.

Chinmay sipped coffee thoughtfully and replied. "True. But we've proven it can be done, and that is enough. Indeed, this is the defining virtue of a constitutional democracy. The politicians are those elected by the people, entrusted with steering this vast ship of the nation. In truth, we have been chosen to partake in this noble endeavour by their discernment. And if our work today bears fruit, the credit must go to those whom the people have elected for this purpose."

He paused for a moment and continued, "Yet, in a more profound sense, the proper credit belongs to those silent visionaries—souls who persist in sowing the seeds of transformation with quiet determination and unwavering hope despite the weight of societal condemnation and resistance. From these seeds, the very genesis of ideological change takes root. And yet, for all their service, they remain destined to the anonymity of the foundation stones.

Ramveer replied. "Remember what Professor Mehta used to tell us at the university? 'Always plant a tree and don't expect shade and fruits from the same tree you have planted."

The two longtime friends paused, absorbing the soothing rhythm of capital's government offices, lights shone late into the night as a new wave of civil servants, moved by their example, persisted in the arduous transformation journey. The government machinery, a colossal, ageing entity developed over many years, was slowly beginning to shift direction, much like an old ship gradually obeying the pull of its rudder.

Persistent resistance loomed on the horizon. Established interests were poised to retaliate, and politicians who had taken credit openly for economic reforms hesitated to continue these reforms as elections neared in respective states. However, a significant transformation had occurred. The potential for genuine, structural, and functional change had been evidenced, at least within government systems. This was regarded as the most significant accomplishment.

From these walls
emerged minds
that moved the world.

GLOBAL ALUMNI
CONCLAVE
ALLAHABAD UNIVERSITY

Igniting Minds | Honoring Roots | Sparking Renaissance

CHAPTER XIII

The Confluence of Minds: An Intellectual Renaissance

Vikram began with quiet determination and a clear vision: to build a bridge between the university's past and its present—to reconnect former students with their alma mater and with one another. A team of dedicated alumni and students, working tirelessly around the clock and engaging all regional and professional chapters, successfully connected a vast network of former students within a year. Under Vikram's astute leadership as Secretary, the association orchestrated numerous intimate gatherings, thought-provoking seminars, and conferences spanning diverse academic disciplines. These events infused the team with extraordinary energy and confidence, emboldening them to envision a grand celebration at their alma mater.

The Association's reach extended to alumni who had ascended to positions of influence throughout the nation, including distinguished civil servants, innovative entrepreneurs, celebrated academics, and visionary leaders across various sectors. Their collective presence promised not merely a reunion but the potential for profound entrepreneurial remoulding.

After extensive consultations with many distinguished Alumni whose names resonated beyond academic circles, the association devised an ingenious system of intellectual exchange. Any former student wishing to engage with current students, faculty, or colleagues on specific topics could have submitted a formal proposal outlining their intended discussion and availability. The association would then circulate this information to the relevant departments, display announcements on campus notice boards, and communicate with other alumni interested in a similar domain.

This elegant mechanism proved extraordinarily successful. Young, aspiring students engaged directly with accomplished professionals who had once walked the same corridors and sat in the same lecture halls. The university became a vibrant nexus where wisdom accumulated through professional experience flowed back to nourish the academic community that had first cultivated it.

After receiving the Vice Chancellor's approval, the Alumni Association planned a magnificent celebration to welcome all Alumni who had graduated since the university's inception. Support poured in from numerous quarters—sister institutions, governmental organisations, media and industrial partners all contributed generously to the grand occasion, each according to their means.

A comprehensive program has been promoted through various media and flyers. The celebration's highlight will be an awards ceremony honouring alumni who exemplify the university's highest ideals through their contributions to society. Among these distinguished individuals are Chinmay and Ramveer, acknowledged not only for their crucial role in steering the nation through economic challenges and fostering sustainable growth but also for their extraordinary personal and professional partnership, which thrived despite the prevailing social norms of their early years.

Chinmay and Ramveer initially hesitated, seeing their accomplishments not as personal triumphs deserving praise but as the inevitable outcomes. After some reflection, they accepted the honour, realising their journey could motivate others.

On the day of celebration, the university grounds teemed with thousands of alumni and students, faculty, distinguished guests, and community members. The state Governor presided over the ceremony with dignified gravitas. When Chinmay's name echoed through the assembly hall, thunderous applause accompanied his path to the stage, where the Governor gave him the award with solemn ceremony. Then came the moment for Chinmay to address the gathering.

Chinmay began with characteristic humility and thoughtfulness:

"Honourable Dignitaries, esteemed Seniors, dear friends, cherished juniors, and the vibrant youth of this transformative institution, I stand before you not as one who claims mastery over our intricate social systems but as a perpetual seeker—an observer captivated by the deeper philosophical currents of life.

I come to you from the heartland of a traditionally vibrant Uttar Pradesh, a village that, despite its structural inequities, embodies Gandhi's vision of Gram Swaraj. In my travels—from the flourishing epicentres of our civilisation to the humble streets awaiting signs of development—I have witnessed patterns that speak to our collective soul, patterns that I know will resonate with each of you, brilliant orators, analytical minds, and creators of tomorrow.

I would like to begin with our beloved childhood; we grew up listening to the timeless episodes of our great epics—the Ramayana and the Mahabharata. These sacred narratives were not mere stories but moral compasses that shaped our inner worlds. There is scarcely a household in which the aspiration has not taken root—that their children may grow to embody the virtues of Lord Rama or the divine wisdom of Lord Krishna. One tale recounts when Lord Rama accepted berries from Sabari, an untouchable, symbolising the breaking of human barriers and honouring divinity.

What more incredible irony can there be than this: for the very untouchable woman whose tasted berries were once savoured by our beloved Lord Ram and whom the Divine embraced with the tender honour of a mother, we rendered her descendants untouchable, barring them from the temples of the same God for centuries?

If God descended upon this earth to manifest the sacred traditions, not by sermons or religious lectures, he illuminated the path of life by walking it himself. For centuries, we have engaged in justifications, interpretations, and propagation of His philosophy of life—yet we have not succeeded in embodying it. Numerous many times more dangerous observations exist across the history of the world where atrocities and genocides taken place in the name of the religions which meant for the peaceful existence of humanity, whether prosecution of Galileo for his heliocentric theory of solar system, Nazi's Holocaust, and Bosnian Genocide.

Our epics and millennia-old history have, time and again, proclaimed this truth with resounding clarity. "While we search for our deities in magnificent and rich temples, gurdwaras, churches, and mosques, they are often found working silently among society's most destitute and marginalised. In the humble struggles of those society has cast aside, we see the seeds of genuine transformation. The divine, it seems, works quietly among the marginalised, urging us to rise above our inherited divisions. I have attempted to understand this from various philosophical perspectives, religious contexts, and modern historical viewpoints."

"What dire consequences befell us for straying from the path Lord Rama and Lord Krishna showed?"

"Can anyone speak on this?" Chinmay asked with curiosity

He paused for a minute; Hall was listening with profound silence.

He then resumed speaking. "We all know this very well. Our sages and religious scholars refer to this era as Kaliyuga—the age of darkness and moral decay. Is this not the same Kaliyuga that our historians perhaps describe as an era of subjugation and servitude under the foreign invaders?"

Intruders and invaders had ravaged, raped and plundered this land of abundance for centuries simply because we failed to adhere to the paths clearly shown by our cherished scriptures in the name of God?

For millennia, the stories of the Mahabharata and the Bhagavata Purana have conveyed a profound truth, narrated initially by a Dalit Sanjay with divine insights: Whenever a ruler, due to attachment, has delegated power to an ineligible individual, the results would have been disastrous. Time and again, society has descended from its peak to its nadir.

Despite knowing, discussing, and even preaching, we have repeatedly made the same mistakes within our families, lineages, and society—just as Dhritarashtra did. What a fierce dilemma our society faces: for centuries, we have proudly echoed Krishna's words—'Change is the law of the world'—yet at the slightest stir of social reform, we cry doom and declare the dawn of Kali Yuga.

Do we still need more reasons for and causes of Kaliyuga or servitude? Or is the answer already woven into our epics and history books?"

After a moment's pause, he resumed confidently: 'We missed connecting our epic with the history of our time. Despite a prolonged and challenging struggle, our democracy gave every community equal opportunity under the law and within the Constitutional framework. As we got this legal power, a few of us started dishonouring these texts or scriptures without fully understanding or analysing them.

Just imagine if we had leveraged the tradition of Shastrārth at our places of worship—an ancient practice of open dialogue that was inclusive of all castes, creeds, and genders. Sacred spaces would have been transformed into open forums, where the moral insights of ancient epics met the rights enshrined in modern constitutions. There, priests, scholars, common people, and skeptics alike would have sat side by side—testing ideas and learning from one another. Such a fusion of age-old wisdom and democratic ideals would have illuminated the path to a more harmonious and equitable society—one in which cultural heritage and fundamental rights reinforced each other.

"After a protracted battle against inner doubts and outward oppression, we finally acheived freedom of speech and expression as a sacred right. Yet in spite of open, earnest debate, a new faction has begun to take shape in our social tapestry—one that brandishes the Constitution as a shield while zealously resisting progress, universal justice and change. Their sporadic outbreaks of aggression strike at the heart of constitutional ideals, without any understanding of its spirit. Just like a few countries adopted Islam as their state religion but executing the contradictory policies to the value enshrined in the Islam- killing innocents, supporting terrorism. Is there anything more derogatory example of blasphemy than this in our time."

Thank you for allowing me to share these reflections with you today. The most incredible honour of my life has not been managing economic recovery but instead applying the wisdom I gained within these walls to serve the collective good. For that opportunity, I remain eternally grateful."

The assembly hall erupted in a thunderous ovation. The audience rose spontaneously, sustaining applause reverberating through the grand space like rolling thunder.

Now came the moment to honour Ramveer—a brilliant mind who had always comfortably assumed a position complementary to Chinmay. This psychological accommodation had been fundamental to their extraordinary partnership. After receiving his award with characteristic grace, Ramveer approached the podium to share his reflections on their remarkable journey.

"Distinguished Governor, honourable ministers, and esteemed scholars, I am deeply honoured to stand before you today and share my reflections.

I must begin by acknowledging that none of my achievements are born of personal brilliance alone; they are the fruit of transformative support, nurtured by a divine spirit that encourages us to rise beyond our inherent limitations.

Imagine society as a living organism—an intricate body made up of countless cells, each with its own vital role. Just as a body needs balanced nourishment and seamless cooperation among its cells to stay healthy, so too does a society depend on the fair distribution of resources and the harmonious functioning of every community.

When a single cell is starved or disabled, disease can spread, weakening the entire body. Likewise, when any social group—be it defined by caste, class, gender, or faith—is denied basic rights or opportunities, it not only suffers but can invite destructive forces that prey on its vulnerability.

History offers stark lessons. In medieval times, the exclusion of Dalits and women from education, civic life, and self-defense left entire kingdoms brittle, unable to withstand invasions or calamities. Practices such as Sati, untouchability, and Johar stand as grim reminders that neglecting even one segment of society risks the health of the whole.

Today, we stand at another crossroads. Human civilisation has reached unprecedented heights—computers in our homes, flights across continents, the decoding of life's very blueprint. Yet rapid progress has cast long shadows: environmental crises, widening inequality, and social unrest. It is not enough to lament these side-effects; we must honor the sacrifices of our ancestors by building a society where material advancement and moral integration go hand in hand.

Nowhere is this challenge more vivid than in our own land. As the world's most diverse nation, we carry a legacy shaped by millennia of pluralism—blending Hindu, Muslim, Sikh, Christian, Jain, and Buddhist traditions into a single social fabric. Our experiment in Sarva Dharma Sambhava—equal reverence for all faiths—and our age-old respect for nature offer a template for a fractured world.

If, in the coming decade, the global community embraces these ideals—uniting ancient wisdom with ecological stewardship and social inclusion—we will redefine civilisation for the planetary age. But if technological prowess outpaces our ethical consciousness, progress will not enlighten but destroy.

The choice before us is clear. Let us nourish every "cell" of society with justice, education, and opportunity. Let us forge harmony out of diversity and let compassion guide our innovations. Only then will we build a future worthy of our shared human legacy—and safeguard our civilisation from ruin."

Ramveer's scientific approach after rational words of Chinmay's, filled the assembly with a tangible sense of intellectual vigour. Among the thousands gathered—students, teachers, dignitaries, and community leaders—many were inspired, hoping to organise similar events in their circles. They left with a determination to create spaces for intellectual discourse in regional educational institutions, aiming to cultivate a collaborative ecosystem that addresses emerging challenges and devises comprehensive, inclusive solutions.

In the crisp afternoon sunlight, an envelope arrived for Chinmay and Ramveer, bearing the old school crest and an invitation. The Old Boys Association of their alma mater was hosting a regional summit on innovation and inclusive development strategies, with a special emphasis on recycling economics. They were to be the Chief Guests at the event – a summit held in commemoration of the peaceful Satyagraha they had once staged at the school gate. As they read the words, they fell silent for a moment, their hearts swelling with pride and disbelief. The once-timid students who had quietly rallied for change now found themselves celebrated as architects of progress. In that instant, they understood that their journey had come full circle. With hearts brimming with hope and quiet triumph, they stepped once again through the school gate, knowing that their voices had been heard and that from the seeds of their courage, a more inclusive and sustainable future lay ahead.

This moment marked not an auspicious beginning of a collective journey toward inclusive creativity—a real renaissance for a subcontinent once celebrated as the "Golden Bird" in the vast chronicles of human civilisation, now poised to reclaim its intellectual heritage and reshape its future trajectory.

Cultural & Contextual Glossary:

Dhritarashtra: In the Hindu epic Mahabharata, Dhritarashtra was the blind king of Hastinapur. He had 100 sons, known as the Kauravas. Duryodhana, his eldest son, was his heir apparent and influenced his decisions, often leading to Dhritarashtra's blind favouritism towards him.

Golden Bird: In ancient times, India's fertile lands, abundant resources, and thriving trade networks made it a global hub for goods and wealth, conferring the name.

The Shastarth: Ancient Indian culture's tradition of debates and dialogue often aimed to clarify the meaning of dharma (Duty) or establish a particular philosophical viewpoint.

The Symphony of Judicious Equilibrium

Decades flowed, layering history with triumphs, trials, victories, and wounds. From forgotten villages to bustling cities, a silent renaissance stirred—the hum of minds unshackled, of institutions once dormant now ignited by purpose. Universities and professional institutes, once symbols of inherited privilege, transformed into vibrant crucibles of discourse, innovation, and inclusion. Their halls echoed with the voices of a generation that understood that justice is not inherited—it must be actively balanced, constantly renewed.

This evolution was the inevitable result of countless acts of courage. Two friends defied history and broke the silence, creating a ripple effect that changed many destinies—across urban and rural areas, suppressed dreams transformed into collaborative creation. As injustice lifted, a conscious shift occurred: inclusive policies, cross-disciplinary innovation, and a culture that valued ideas over lineage.

The ancient wisdom of interconnectedness—"Vasudhaiva Kutumbakam" (the world is one family)—found a new voice in this grand balancing act. It merged with the precision of modern systems, forging an ethos where diversity was strength and compassion was the strategy. Social inclusion was no longer an aspiration deferred to tomorrow; it became today's reality—proof that society could heal itself without fracture when conscious of its imbalances.

The story of Ramveer and Chinmay guides societies in transition, highlighting that unresolved injustice can lead to turmoil. However, when confronted with courage and conscience, it can foster renewal. Their small acts of fairness multiplied over time, transforming scars into symbols of resilience rather than regret.

As we close this chapter, the whisper they left behind grows louder—a call to all who inherit a divided world: Justice is not a gift bestowed from above; it is the delicate, daily work of minds awoken to inequality and hearts alert to humanity. Balance is not a passive equilibrium; it is a living effort—measured in questions asked, opportunities extended, and barriers dismantled.

The legacy of these two friends reminds us that we do not build the future by destiny alone—it is shaped, recalibrated, and redeemed by the steady hands of justice, generation after generation.